Dante looked at her narrowly for a few seconds.

"Personally, I am utterly disinterested in marriage. I've been married once and it's an institution I have since resolved never to venture near again."

Kate nodded. He'd loved and lost. In his office, a dramatic painting of the flamboyant, haughty beauty hung behind his desk, a testament to an irreplaceable love.

"But you said..."

"I don't want to marry, Kate. I intend to. Those are two quite separate propositions, and do I have a suitable candidate in mind? Yes, I do. She is sitting in this kitchen with me. I've asked you here, Kate, for your hand in marriage..."

Cathy Williams can remember reading Harlequin books as a teenager, and now that she is writing them, she remains an avid fan. For her, there is nothing like creating romantic stories and engaging plots, and each and every book is a new adventure. Cathy lives in London, and her three daughters—Charlotte, Olivia and Emma—have always been, and continue to be, the greatest inspirations in her life.

Books by Cathy Williams

Harlequin Presents

Desert King's Surprise Love-Child
Consequences of Their Wedding Charade
Hired by the Forbidden Italian
Bound by a Nine-Month Confession
A Week with the Forbidden Greek
The Housekeeper's Invitation to Italy
The Italian's Innocent Cinderella

Secrets of the Stowe Family

Forbidden Hawaiian Nights
Promoted to the Italian's Fiancée
Claiming His Cinderella Secretary

Visit the Author Profile page
at Harlequin.com for more titles.

Cathy Williams

UNVEILED AS THE ITALIAN'S BRIDE

HARLEQUIN
PRESENTS

Recycling programs
for this product may
not exist in your area.

ISBN-13: 978-1-335-59180-7

Unveiled as the Italian's Bride

Harlequin Enterprises ULC
22 Adelaide St. West, 41st Floor
Toronto, Ontario M5H 4E3, Canada
www.Harlequin.com

Printed in U.S.A.

UNVEILED AS THE ITALIAN'S BRIDE

CHAPTER ONE

'DANTE, MY BOY, it is time for you to marry once again. The time has come.'

Antonio D'Agostino's hands fluttered, his eyes dampened, his mouth wobbled and he reached for the linen napkin at the side of his plate, which he pressed over his eyes for a few fraught seconds.

Summoned from Milan to his uncle's palace near Venice, Dante watched this emotional spectacle with an element of wry scepticism. Antonio had been circling round this thorny subject for years, delicately sidestepping any outright conversations on the matter, content to lob arrows over a wall and hope one of them landed.

Now Dante sat back, pushed his plate to one side, adjusted his chair and stretched his long legs.

He was quite accustomed to his uncle's emotionalism. Antonio D'Agostino could weep for Italy at the drop of a hat. He had shed tears over everything from the plight of displaced people to the fate of stray dogs. He was the polar opposite of Dante's parents and Dante loved him for that.

Growing up, Dante's uncle had been the one who had opened his eyes to the fact that life could actually be fun. Born into Italian nobility, both his parents had been the epitome of duty. Their aristocratic ancestry had come with obligations They had never allowed themselves to forget that and neither had they ever let *him* forget it. It was drummed into his DNA, embedded from the day he'd been born, invisible chains around his ankles from the very day he'd been old enough to walk.

Until the day they'd died—being driven to the opera on a rain-drenched, foggy evening, taking his ex-wife, Luciana, with them in an accident that had changed the course of Dante's life for ever— they had never once, strayed from what had been expected of them.

Vast estates were there to be managed… They had mixed with the right people, who all lived in the right places and had the right amount of blue blood running through their veins.

Anything else would have been unacceptable.

And for Dante, their only child, they had done their very best to position him on the same road down which they had spent their lives travelling. They had failed to factor in an irreverent, fun-loving, globe-trotting uncle who would probably have spent his lifetime living it up on his substantial inheritance had it not been for Efisio's and Sofia's deaths.

At this point, he had become the majority shareholder, thanks to Dante having relinquished much of his stake in the company years previously to focus on his own substantial holdings. Antonio had fed considerable money into the family empire and, in return, Dante had the freedom to hold the reins of his own holdings without having to split the very little time he always seemed to have at his disposal.

'You know how I feel about…marriage,' Dante said warily, but there was an undercurrent of warning in his voice, a reminder that this was a subject not open to discussion. 'And, Antonio, tears aren't going to get me to have a rethink on this. Marriage? It's a place I have no intention of ever revisiting.'

Antonio sniffed and rang the bell for their food to be taken away.

Dinner had been served in the smaller of the dining rooms, which was still a stunning marvel of chandeliers, frescoes and ornate turquoise-and-gold wallpaper, only interrupted by four sprawling paintings of the Venetian canals.

Dante had no idea where this conversation was going but fondness for his uncle prevented him from summarily dismissing the conversation out of hand. He would politely hear him out and *then* dismiss the conversation out of hand.

'We should have a brandy.' Antonio got to his feet as soon as the dishes had been cleared away. 'I have work to do before I retire.'

Antonio waved aside the objection.

'How often do you make it to Venice, Dante, to visit your frail, old uncle? Once a year?'

'Once every six weeks,' Dante returned drily. 'And let's not forget summer, when I'm here every week for at least a couple of days at a time, sweltering in the heat and battling the crowds every time I get up the courage to venture into the city.'

'Work, work, work.' Antonio waved dismissively, 'You'd better take my arm, Dante. I'm not a young man any more.'

'You're hardly ancient at seventy-two…' But Dante obligingly supported the much shorter man as they made their way out of the dining room and towards one of the sitting rooms, favoured by his uncle because it overlooked the finest of the manicured gardens to the side of the palace.

Was it his imagination or had his uncle shed some weight? If so, it would do him no harm. If Antonio was fond of passing dark judgement on his nephew's life choices, then Dante was equally outspoken about his uncle's penchant for rich food, every morsel of which seemed to settle around his waist.

'I am not going to be distracted this time, Dante. I mean what I say. It is time for you to marry. It is time for you to put Luciana behind you. I realise you still love her but she has been gone now for over four years and Angelina needs a mother.'

Dante stiffened. He was outraged and taken

aback in equal measure by his uncle's full-frontal invasion of his privacy. Diplomacy had been jettisoned and there was not a single syllable in Antonio's remark that he didn't find offensive.

He remained silent.

Emotionalism might be his uncle's familiar terrain but it very much was not his. A rigorously unemotional upbringing had left no room inside him for that. That said, he was guarded and still as they entered the grand sitting room.

The palace might have been compact, compared to other grand Italian estates but it was still enormous and furnished with a level of ornateness beloved by his flamboyant uncle. Here, two of the walls were a dramatic red, and a lifetime of travelling the world was there for all to appreciate in the form of anything and everything that had been collected along the way. A statuesque African marble tribal priestess held court on a Persian rug of finest silk, framed by two exquisite watercolours from the Far East. Dante was pretty sure this was a one off, as the interior of palaces went.

'So…' He opened the conversation as he moved to sit on one of the deep chairs. 'Can I ask what's brought about this sudden urgency for me to find a wife?'

His eyes were drawn to a pair of curling, hand-crafted wooden snakes crawling along the wall, a souvenir from a trip to Mexico a million years ago.

He turned his attention back to his uncle, who

had sunk into the chair facing Dante and was now fumbling in his trouser pocket to whip out a crumpled piece of paper, which he thrust into Dante's hand. His eyes, once more, were welling up.

'What's brought this on? I'm giving up running all this, Dante.' He waved to encompass the room, the palace and beyond. 'The land, the estates, the properties: all of it. Even this place—too big for an old man like me. I know Efisio respected your desire to step back from active participation in the family business, but I have reached the end of the line, and I need you now. I ran away from my duties as a boy and returned to them when I had to, as a man, when Efisio died. I have enjoyed the journey in my old age, but no more.'

He cleared his throat. 'And read the letter. Go on. It's from my consultant in Venice. I'm dying, Dante, so *that's* why you need to marry. Someone by your side when you take over. How can I face my maker knowing that you're still drifting? That Angelina is without a mother? That you remain in the grip of the past? Not to mention the fact that you will have to be more present in the running of the family empire, and you know as well as I do that they are all traditionalists. I have had to listen daily to your various relatives ask me when you're going to settle down once again.'

'Forget about my conservative relatives! I can handle their curiosity. But what's all this nonsense about meeting your maker? Since when are you dying? What the hell are you talking about?'

But Dante's hand was trembling as he unfolded the official letter and read it, then read it again, his panic only steadying when he began to decipher the glimmers of optimism in the diagnosis.

'You never told me that you were worried about your prostate, Antonio,' he admonished grimly.

'You're a busy man. Why would I worry you?'

'I will telephone this consultant first thing in the morning.'

'You will do no such thing! I can handle this.'

'You're spinning tales of meeting your maker and you haven't even heard what the prognosis is.'

'I need treatment. You read it! They've done tests. They need to do more!'

'No one seems to be panicking.'

'I'm panicking! My life is over and I want to leave it safe in the knowledge that my favourite nephew—'

'Your only nephew'

'Is married. You have lots of fine words about never marrying again, but I love Angelina, and what lies ahead of her without the guiding hand of a mother? The child is young now, but time marches on. I've kept my thoughts on this to myself but this death sentence…' His eyes welled up.

'You need to stop talking about death sentences, Antonio. This is not the time for high drama. What are these various tests you've been having?' But Dante's mind was in a whirl as he was forced to confront a situation he had known was hibernating in the shadows. Antonio, reluctant though he was to admit it, had a point. He didn't see enough of his daughter and, whilst she had everything that only vast wealth could buy, he really had no idea how to plait hair, pick out matching pink outfits or answer questions about nail polish. She was sweet-natured, gentle and undemanding, none of which made his guilt any less burdensome.

Antonio was scared, and fear had propelled him into voicing deep concerns to which he had previously only alluded, and those concerns were not entirely baseless. The bottom line was that his uncle felt that he was now facing his own mortality, and whether he was right or wrong on that front was immaterial.

'I can hardly conjure up a suitable wife from thin air,' Dante mused, folding the letter and setting it down on the table between them.

'But you can think about it—think about settling down. There are many lovely young women out there, if you would open your eyes. It would make a dying old fool so happy…'

Dante reached for the handkerchief and handed it to his uncle. A steady supply of them was always a must when visiting. He watched in silence as Antonio dabbed his eyes, visibly more relaxed now that his worrying news had been imparted.

'You need to stop playing the death card, Antonio. I've read the letter and, yes, it's not a bad thing to be concerned. But if you filter through the technical terms and make your way past the medical terminology, you can see that this is not a terminal situation being described.'

He would reassure his uncle, but he could detect real anxiety on Antonio's face, and Dante loved his uncle. He loved him in ways he had never loved his own remote and aloof father. Loved him for the way he'd occasionally swept in to rescue him from his boarding school routine, whipping him out for a weekend to see a football match or a play, where afterwards they'd hobnobbed with the actors backstage, because Antonio seemed to know them all. Life in his gilded cage had been joyless. His uncle had been the only one occasionally to open the bars of that cage and show him what was possible outside.

So Antonio was after him to get married. Well, was there anything he wouldn't do for Antonio? He would oblige.

Dante relaxed. The sickening panic that had gripped him began to fade and he began to think as he always did: rationally; coolly; unemotionally. All things were possible when you eliminated emotion from the equation. Life had taught him that from a very young age. Rely on cold logic and you never lost your way. Yes, his uncle had opened pages in which life was painted in many different hues, a life of freedom and adventure.

But, for Dante, those pictures were snapshots of a life anchored in the more serious, unrelenting business of hard work and duty. He loved Antonio but he had never been persuaded into emulating him. Perhaps, he often mused, DNA trumped everything. So now…marriage? He knew just the woman to walk down the aisle with him.

He smiled a slow, leisurely, obliging smile and gave just the slightest of shrugs.

'You win.' He held up both hands in a gesture of surrender and Antonio's eyebrows shot up.

'You will think about settling down? For my sake?'

'I will.' Dante tilted his head to one side. 'But there's no such thing as a free lunch, old man. I get to engage with your consultant, no holds barred, from tomorrow and there will be no decision made, no appointment taken without me by your side. Agreed?'

Antonio leant back in the chair, closed his eyes and smiled.

'Agreed…'

Kate was not expecting Dante to return for at least another three days. He had gone to Venice to see his uncle and would then be flying to New York on business.

Could she manage?

It had been one of those polite questions not in search of an answer, because she was very much used to managing in his absence. Wasn't she? She had smiled back with equal politeness and told him that of course she could manage.

She had now been working for him for over two years and she would have staked her life that she knew his eight-year-old daughter, Angelina, a darn sight better than he knew her himself because he was so seldom around.

He swept in when work allowed him and spent some quality time with his daughter—which usually took the form of collecting her from her prestigious day school in Milan and treating her to a mega-expensive meal out somewhere before depositing her back at home base, job done.

At least twice a month, he had a formal briefing with Kate for updates on Angelina's schooling. Kate had no idea how he formatted the school holidays, when she was released from duties, free to do as she wished. But, from everything her little charge had told her, he just swapped one nanny for another—Kate, who was there for most of the year, and her replacement, for when she disappeared for the very generous holidays she'd been given as part of her package.

Angelina adored him. She clung to those little moments together and held them close like treasures. The year before, he had attended her nativity play and she had been unspeakably excited for him to be in the audience.

Yet, from Kate's point of view, he was cold, distant and far too absent from his daughter's life.

He was also way more good-looking than he had any right to be, and so eye-wateringly rich and crazily sophisticated that he always managed to make her feel self-conscious and deeply uncomfortable.

But every single criticism of the man was overshadowed by the handsome amount she was paid at the end of the month. Not only were the perks of the job staggering but there was no way she could ever have earned what she had over the past two years anywhere else in the world.

And she needed the money.

Still...

It was a little after eight in the evening. Kate was curled up on the sofa in the sitting area—just part of her suite of rooms in his vast mansion on the outskirts of Milan—and she wasn't expecting him back. She picked up her mobile, stomach clenching as she heard his accented, deep drawl down the end of the line, politely asking her whether it was too late for him to have a word with her.

'I—where?' Kate was confused. 'I thought you were—um—in New York...'

'It's unlikely I would be asking you to meet me

if I were in New York. I'm in the kitchen. I've just arrived back in Milan.'

'Right.'

'I take it that Angelina is asleep? No, no need to answer that. I'll find out how her day has been when I see you. Fifteen minutes? Will that work for you?'

'Of course.'

No time to change. Her day uniform was always reasonably formal, not because there had ever been any restrictions on what she wore but because she felt it was appropriate. Right now, cold as it was with Milan fully in the grip of winter, her uniform comprised woollen skirts, tights and sensible jumpers.

She glanced down at the faded jeans and the old rugby shirt given to her by her father ages ago—although where on earth he could possibly have got it was a mystery—and hurriedly tidied her hair, pausing as she passed the ornate, full-length mirror by the door.

Twenty-four years old, five-seven, slight in build, straight, shoulder-length brown hair, regular features… She wondered if this was why he always made her feel so self-conscious. He was so ridiculously good-looking and next to him she always managed to end up feeling as exotic as a sparrow.

When she'd first come to work for him, the house had felt bewilderingly large. After two years, she was familiar with its layout, though all the marble, columns and swirling staircases that separated the various wings never failed to impress her.

She hurried down to the kitchen but, when she reached the door, she paused and took a few deep breaths.

She was composed as she pushed open the door and padded into the kitchen, hovering indecisively for a few seconds, waiting for him to look at her. He was staring out of the window at a bleak November night and, when he finally turned, his dark eyes were opaque, his expression unreadable.

Kate did her utmost to control the rush of heat that engulfed her. Every time she saw him, it was as though she was seeing him for the first time, captivated all over again by his swarthy beauty. He was well over six feet, his hair midnight-black and cropped short, his aristocratic features sharply, exquisitely perfect, his body lean and muscled.

'I hope I didn't interfere with your evening.' Dante nodded to a bottle of red on the marble kitchen counter but his dark eyes didn't stray from her face. 'Join me in a drink?'

'No. Thank you.'

'You can sit, Kate, and there's no need to look quite so nervous. You're not about to be reprimanded for something you may have forgotten you've done. How is Angelina? How were the tests she took two days ago?'

'Great. She's had some excellent results in her maths and English and, in fact, she was asked to read her essay out loud for the class. Her Christmas play is the week after next and I wonder if you've perhaps decided whether you can come or not...?'

'I see no reason why not. I'll get my PA to clear my diary for the day, although naturally I can't promise anything.' He swirled his glass and stared down into the deep red liquid for a few seconds, then looked at her in silence.

This woman had worked for him for a little over two years and he knew next to nothing about her personal life. Not that he had ever had much interest in digging deep. She was highly competent, Angelina adored her and she kept herself to herself. What else could possibly be relevant?

He was well trained when it came to drawing very clear lines between himself and his employees but, even so, there had always been something resting in the shadows that drew his reluctant eyes to places they didn't belong. To the slender gracefulness of her figure, to the smooth calm of her features and to barely-there hints of undercurrents that belied that calm exterior.

'She'll be thrilled.' Kate smiled and met his gaze. 'She's always very excited when you attend school events.'

Dante wondered, just fleetingly, whether there

was an implied criticism there and then decided that there wasn't.

'I expect you must be wondering why I've asked to have a chat with you.'

'Well,' Kate returned cautiously, 'Not at all. I work for you and—and—naturally you're going to want to find out how Angelina is, how her day's been…'

'I've just been to see my uncle.'

'How is he?' This time Kate's smile was genuine. She was very fond of Antonio. She and Angelina would often visit, sometimes at the beginning of the summer holidays before Kate returned to England, sometimes during Angelina's half terms. How on earth he could be related to Dante was a mystery because, as personalities went, they couldn't have been more different.

'Not well, I'm afraid to say.'

'My word, what's the matter with him?'

'To be blunt, he's been diagnosed with possible cancer. Nothing's confirmed but the signs bear thinking about.' Dante held up one hand as though to stop a possible interruption even though Kate's mouth had dropped open in speechless, horrified silence. 'I personally don't think that it's nearly as serious as he seems to believe, but he's fairly frantic with worry. I've spent the past day and a half with him, going to see his consultant so that I can get a clear picture of what exactly is going on.'

'And…?'

'More tests need to be done. Things aren't as clear cut as they might have assumed, given all the physical symptoms, but there were certainly no murmurings of doom.' Dante stared at the drink, took a sip and sighed. 'Unfortunately, things aren't quite as straightforward in other areas as could be expected.'

'What do you mean?'

'Antonio seems to think that this diagnosis places him at death's door, despite reassurances from myself and from his consultant. He's managed to convince himself that the Grim Reaper is lurking around the corner and he's now in the process of putting his affairs in order.'

'What does that mean?'

'It means, firstly, that he's going to give up overall running of the family estates. Frankly, much of the business of running the estates is already extensively handled by people I put in place when my parents died, and before Antonio assumed full control, but it's a big deal for him. He's going to leave the palace and is making noises about retiring to the countryside, even though there's absolutely no need for such a drastic change.'

'I guess the palace *is* very big for a man on his own.'

Dante frowned.

'What does size have to do with it?'

'He might feel a little lonely, I guess…'

'This place is not much smaller. I've never felt lonely in it.'

Kate shrugged and gazed down at her fingers linked on her lap.

What a world Dante D'Agostino inhabited. One in which palaces, castles, vineyards and villas were all just part and parcel of an accepted lifestyle. Was it even possible for him to stop and consider that an old man might just find a palace something of a handful, even if all his needs *were* catered for?

She thought of some of the places she had lived in with her parents, forever travelling across the country, dipping into Europe now and again, jumping from mobile home to canal boat to the occasional caravan thrown in for good measure. One of the most permanent places had been a commune in Scotland, where they had lived for over two years, during which time Kate had thrived, caught up on her schooling and enjoyed the temporary bliss of having roots in one place.

Her hippy parents had never contemplated the horror of settling down in one place. She couldn't remember a time when she had lived in any place bigger than a handful of rooms and where getting on top of one another had been part of the deal. Home tutoring had joined forces with conventional education now and again, and she had just had to make the best of it in all the weird and wacky places they had stayed in.

And here she was with a guy who couldn't see why a palace to house one person might be a bit over the top.

'Why are you smiling?'

'Was I?' Kate blinked and looked at Dante and, for a few seconds, the breath caught in her throat because he was so close to her, close enough for her to fall into the dark depths of his eyes which made her feel oxygen-deprived.

'He's considering bee-keeping as his new hobby,' Dante imparted with a frustrated gesture. 'I have no idea where that came from. I believe he watched a documentary a few days ago… Look, the point is, he's having a re-evaluation of his way forward and that seems to involve several…what can I say…?'

He defaulted into Italian and, fluent though Kate now was, she couldn't quite keep up with whatever he was trying to say. Whatever it was, he wasn't comfortable with it, and she felt just the slightest twinge of unease.

He'd told her that there was nothing to worry about, that she wasn't going to be reprimanded, but what if this impromptu meeting was to sack her? Or perhaps just *let her go*, maybe with a sympathetic golden handshake?

Kate was suddenly clammy with panic. She depended on this income and the prospect of having it whipped away filled her with fear. Two and a half years ago, her father had had an accident on his damned motorbike. He was in his fifties and yet still fancied himself a young buck, with his fast bike which always seemed to take precedence over the rusting old car her mother preferred to use.

It had been horrific. He had lost a leg in the accident and, at that point, the travelling days had come to an abrupt end. Her father, always the most genial of guys, always ready for a joke, a sweet-natured bear who'd have done anything for anyone, had plunged headlong into a crippling depression.

The change to their lifestyle, the intense months of physio, and the loss of all those occasional earnings that had kept them afloat had all been too much.

As well the shame. Her dad had had to face the lack of time and thought he had put into their future, always living in the moment. With little to fall back on, he had been overwhelmed by a sense of failure, and it had been heart-breaking.

At the time, Kate had just started teaching at a primary school in Windsor. Her parents had rented themselves a mobile home by the coast and had been planning to stay in one spot for the duration of summer.

Her mother would sell the jewellery she made at Christmas fairs and her dad would find work at one of the local nurseries. He was a talented landscape gardener with an encyclopaedic knowledge of plants.

The accident had put paid to everything.

Her mother had been strong and supportive but there was no way a mobile home was going to be sufficient. For the first time in their lives, they had been forced to face the prospect of bidding a permanent farewell to their travelling days.

They had no money saved to speak of, no pension set aside for a rainy day and an indefinite wait for the sort of intense physio her dad needed—and never mind his mental health, which had been in a sorry state.

Her wonderful, free-living parents had needed more than just cups of tea and sympathy. They had needed hard cash. They had needed money for a house that could be adapted, for a dedicated physiotherapist, for someone to help get her dad's head back in the right place and to take the stress and strain off her mother's shoulders.

And then this job had been advertised. Kate had applied on a whim because it had hinted at a good package. She had got it and the package was stupendous.

What the heck would she do without it?

There were still all sorts of things eating up the money she sent over every single month. She had been able to put down a deposit on a tiny place in Lancashire for them but there was still a mortgage to be paid off. Physically, her father's recovery had been all they could have hoped for, but he was still prone to bouts of depression, so still saw his lovely therapist once a week.

Then there was the business of them earning money. They were still relatively young. She had set up a cottage industry for her mother to pursue her jewellery-making on a bigger scale, which was going well. The house had a fair amount of land and, at some expense, Kate had developed an acre of it into crops that her father could harvest for their own consumption and to sell locally. Everything took money and, amongst all of this expenditure, she herself still had to save money for her own place at some point.

She whitened as a future scenario unravelled in her head, taking a wrecking ball to dreams and expectations she now knew she had been stupid to bank on. How long had she reasonably expected this job to last—for ever? How could she not have factored in the obvious, which was that everyone was expendable, and no more so than a young teacher who had landed the plum post through sheer luck—or something. She had never quite worked that one out.

She tucked her hair behind her ears and realised that her hands were shaking.

'I know what this is about,' she said, clearing her throat, determined to deal with the elephant in the room before it stampeded all over her. Circumstances had made her strong. A peripatetic lifestyle had toughened her, forged an independence in her, because she had never had the luxury of the same faces, the same friends, around her growing up. Her father's accident and everything that had happened subsequently had only served to make her stronger.

But right now she felt weak.

'I very much doubt that,' Dante murmured truthfully.

'When somebody close to you falls ill, everything changes. Your uncle is ill and you—you've had a rethink about Angelina and her future.'

'I have? Hmm…maybe so, in a manner of speaking…'

Kate chewed her lip and tried hard to summon up all that strength and energy she had always been able to fall back on but those reserves were proving hard to locate.

'You no longer need my services.'

She looked away because she was terrified of seeing confirmation of that blunt statement in his eyes. The silence stretched.

'Interesting deduction, but you're very wide of the mark with that one,' Dante drawled eventually.

'What do you mean?'

'Perhaps you should have something to drink before I say what I have called you here to say.'

He didn't wait for her to respond, instead moving to fetch another wine glass and then proceeding to pour her some of the red wine, before sitting back and looking at her with deadly seriousness.

Kate smiled weakly. He was being so polite, so controlled, yet he was still so forbidding.

She gulped down a mouthful of the red and welcomed the rush of alcohol to her head.

'Along with the sudden desire to move house and the new-found interest in bee-keeping, my uncle...' He hesitated and then said on an exasperated sigh, 'Has got it into his head that it is time for me to find myself a wife and settle down.'

'Oh. Well...'

'Surprised?'

'It's not something that he's ever mentioned to me,' Kate said in confusion. 'And I have no thoughts on that one way or another.'

The man might be sinfully good-looking, and with a pedigree that would have every eligible woman in the country pulling tickets to join a queue for the role of *wife,* but Kate had no idea, because his private life had always been private. In all her time working for Dante, she had never known him bring back any woman or introduce his daughter to anyone who was potential wife material.

That said, he was away an extraordinary amount, and probably had a wild and raunchy life somewhere else.

The thought of which brought hectic colour to Kate's cheeks and, when she slid a look at him from under her lashes, it was to find him staring at her with his head tilted to one side. He didn't have to utter a word to press all sorts of crazy buttons inside her.

'At any rate, he's got it into his head that he's on the way out, and he can't possible depart this mortal coil without seeing me settled with a suitable woman.'

'And is there...er...a suitable woman around?' Kate asked while she busily wondered where this was heading.

'In actual fact, there is,' Dante murmured.

'Oh.'

'This is why you're here and why we're having this conversation, as it happens. The truth of the matter is I care very deeply for my uncle, and my fear is that stress and worry will propel him to the early grave he's convinced awaits him when there is no reason why he shouldn't outlive us all, with suitable treatment.'

'I understand,' Kate returned with heartfelt honesty as she thought of her own father and the depression that had consumed him after his accident.

Dante looked at her narrowly for a few seconds. 'Do you?' He paused and shrugged. 'No matter. Personally, I am utterly uninterested in marriage. I've been married once and it's an institution I have since resolved never to venture near again.'

Kate nodded. He'd loved and lost. In his office,

a dramatic painting of the flamboyant, haughty beauty hung behind his desk, a testament to an irreplaceable love.

'But you said…'

'I don't *want* to marry, Kate. I *intend* to. Those are two quite separate propositions. And do I have a suitable candidate in mind? Yes, I do. She is sitting in this kitchen with me. I've asked you here, Kate, for your hand in marriage.'

CHAPTER TWO

FOR A FEW SECONDS, a crazy, dizzying thought spun through Kate's head. She'd *actually* thought that the guy sitting opposite her had asked her to marry him!

Since she had clearly misheard, she pinned a frozen, polite smile to her face and looked at him quizzically.

What was there to say? She blinked like a rabbit caught in headlights and waited for clarification.

'You're not following, are you?' Dante said drily. 'I don't blame you.'

'I'm sorry. I really don't understand what's going on.'

'My uncle…'

'I get the bit about your uncle. The bit I *don't* get is the bit that came afterwards.'

'It's simple. Antonio is in a fragile place. He's desperate for me to marry. He has been for some time, but only now has the suggestion broken the surface and been voiced outright. I did what I could over the past couple of days to reassure him that this is not the terminal situation he fears, but...'

Dante raked his fingers through his hair and, in that instant, Kate saw something she had never seen before—she saw his humanity and a love for his uncle that had been called to account and held up to scrutiny.

Which brought her no closer to understanding what was going on. She eyed the bottle and wondered whether another glass was called for or whether a steady head was what was needed.

'If marriage is what he wants, if it can help him navigate this temporary setback, then marriage is what I will give him.'

'But *me*? Signor D'Agostino...'

'Dante.'

Kate skirted around that informality. 'Why me?'

Her head had not stopped spinning. She realised that she was leaning forward, every muscle tense with strain, her whole body in a state of shock.

'It's simple.'

'*Simple?*' She wondered whether they were on the same planet. She'd always known that this was a man who lived in a different realm from her and most other people. He breathed the rarefied air of someone who led a life of extreme wealth and privilege, accustomed to servitude and obedience, but surely their worlds were not so badly aligned that he could actually think that asking a perfect stranger for her hand in marriage was *simple*?

'Like I said, I've already been married.' His face darkened and he glanced down before raising cool, midnight-dark eyes back to her face. 'I will not be going there again in any way that is meaningful. I do not want a woman who thinks that there will be love involved, or anything else for that matter. All doors to any relationship along those lines were shut a long time ago.'

'Anything else?' Kate asked faintly, her brows knitted as she tried to keep pace with what he was telling her.

'Think hard about that one,' Dante drawled wryly, 'And I'm sure you'll get my drift.'

He sat back and sipped his wine while Kate absorbed exactly what that remark meant.

A marriage without love or sex for the sake of his uncle… The colour drained away from her face and her mouth fell open.

'I want a woman I can communicate with,' he said with deadly seriousness. 'And one who is guaranteed to get along with my daughter. Angelina is as central to this as my uncle is. I also want someone who knows exactly how the ground lies and will not complicate matters by thinking that there will ever be anything more to the arrangement than what's on the table.'

'And you think *I* fit the bill?' Kate queried incredulously. 'What you're proposing… Look, I'm sorry, but you're going to have to find someone else to fill the role...'

'Because this doesn't tally with your romantic vision of what a marriage should look like?'

'That amongst a thousand other reasons!'

Dante allowed the silence to fill the space between them. This was the first time any conversation between them had strayed out of safe territory.

He had regular face-to-face meetings with her, was always pleased with what she had to say about Angelina and even more pleased with what Angelina had to say about her. She maintained an excellent balance between discipline and fun, probably because she was young and lively. She and Angelina did a great deal together and, whenever he took his daughter out to lunch or dinner, he was always treated to enthusiastic reports of picnics had, galleries visited, concerts attended or biscuits baked.

But, for the first time, she was no longer in her comfort zone and he was seeing aspects to her that had not previously been apparent. The convenient image was shifting and what was swimming into focus was something different. He was seeing a fiery independence that didn't quite tally with the 'eyes down', reserved woman who sometimes answered his questions so quietly that he had to strain to hear her. The woman who never entered his office for their briefings without a uniform of neatly ironed skirts or trousers, and blouses that were invariably buttoned to the neck.

Shuttered eyes briefly took in what she was wearing now, old, worn clothes that did wonders for her slender, boyish figure and a face that was oddly appealing as she stared at him with flushed cheeks and defiant, glittering hazel eyes. He'd seen her before—of course he had—but he was *seeing* her now and something stirred inside him, a dangerous sizzle that he stamped down with ruthless efficiency so that it barely registered on his consciousness.

'Two years,' he said abruptly.

'I beg your pardon?'

'Marriage for two years—after which you will be free to go your own way.'

'Absolutely not!' Kate sprang to her feet and glared at him, furious that in the midst of this bizarre conversation he remained as cool as a cucumber.

But then the man was so cold—so chillingly contained. His interactions with his daughter were so formal compared to her own relationship with her parents. She knew that he loved Angelina as much as Angelina adored him and had seen flashes of it now and again when he had smiled at something or quizzed her about something she might have said. Who knew? Perhaps during those lunches and dinners, when the pair of them went out, he was a different man but Kate doubted it.

'Sit back down. Please. This conversation is far from over.'

'It is for me,' Kate told him quietly but her legs were wobbly and she remained where she was, hovering.

'I have not got to the crux of this.'

Naturally, she thought, she was not interested in the crux of anything. His proposition was insane. Perhaps this was how Italian nobility behaved, with complete disregard for the sort of basic codes of behaviour that most normal people adhered to.

'I'm really not interested.' Yet she still dithered on the spot, held captive by the cool, calm assurance in his eyes.

'Marriage will come with…some eye-watering advantages.'

'Really? I'm doubting that very much.'

'Two years and you leave with a fortune big enough to keep you in whatever lifestyle you desire for the rest of your life.'

'I'm not interested in…feathering my nest,' Kate stumbled.

'Sure about that? Because you were the only candidate interviewed for this job who was honest enough to tell my panel the real reason you were interested in taking it.'

Kate felt slow, burning colour scorch her cheeks. She could remember that interview as clearly as if it had been yesterday. Three interviewers sitting opposite her, very charming and very encouraging, each equipped with questions about her proficiency, her qualifications, her expectations and her willingness to live abroad.

They had quizzed her on possible scenarios and asked her how she would handle certain situations. She had been told that there would be a bodyguard present in certain instances. Was she comfortable with that?

Kate had been unfazed. She'd had too much on her mind just then to be nervous and had already predicted that she wouldn't get the job anyway. Had she cared? Her father had been in hospital, facing the prospect of his life being turned on its head. Neither he nor her mother had put down sufficient roots. Money was going to be an issue. Problems coming from all directions had piled up in droves, and her head was far too cloudy with anxiety and unhappiness for her worries over a job interview to find a foothold.

Their final question, delivered with the same inscrutable politeness, had been why she wanted the job and Kate had taken a deep breath and answered truthfully.

'The money.'

All three had glanced at one another with barely concealed expressions of shock, at which point she had weakly tacked on something more conciliatory about the challenges of dealing with a charge on a one-to-one basis, where input would be all the more essential, and the desire to improve her stumbling Italian.

She had got the job.

'You wanted the money,' Dante reminded her and then he allowed her to stew in her own mortified silence for a couple of minutes.

'I suppose that was faithfully reported back to you by the people who interviewed me?'

'I had transcripts and recordings of every word said.'

'I see. Why did you choose to give me the job, in that case? Can I ask?'

'Because I appreciated your honesty. You were the only one to mention the amount the job was going to be paying, even though I'd wager that every single one of your competitors was thinking the same thing. I like to know where people stand. No room for misunderstandings.'

'But…'

'I also liked the way you dealt with certain test cases presented to you. Plus, you were young— young enough for Angelina not to see you as a teacher, waiting for her to return from school to pick up where she had left off with the learning.'

'Why didn't you conduct the interviews yourself?'

'Because…' Dante leant forward and smiled slowly. It was a smile that sent a spiral of something hot and unexpected curling through her.

'It's my experience that, for better or for worse, I can sometimes have an effect on people, and that would have been detrimental to the interviewing process in my opinion.'

Kate knew exactly where he was going with that remark. Of course he would know just the sort of effect he risked having on any prospective candidates. He was a guy who scrambled brains. She had seen the way people jumped at his command, the way cool, self-assured people stumbled into speech when he addressed them, the way nerves seemed to paralyse their ability to think on the spot. Had he wanted the people being interviewed to lose the power of speech every time he asked a question?

Which brought her right back to his proposition, and to the twist in the conversation, because he had done his due diligence and had found her Achilles' heel.

'I have no idea why you need the money,' he admitted with an exotic gesture that spoke volumes. 'I could have dug a bit deeper, but how you choose to spend what you earn is your business. I had sufficient information at my disposal to offer you the position, including naturally a comprehensive criminal background check.'

Kate didn't care about background checks; they were standard procedure. She was, however, aghast that he might have investigated her private

life which, as far as she was concerned, was beyond the pale.

'That's just awful,' she told him bluntly and
Dante frowned.

'What?'

'Everything. This! All of it. A marriage proposal like this—putting money on the table as
though it buys everything and everyone. The way
you casually mention that you could have pried
into my private life without my knowledge!'

Dante flushed darkly.

All the fire and passion that had been conspic-
uously absent on the many occasions when they
had had their debriefings was in evidence now.
Her eyes flashed and there was vivid colour stain-
ing her cheeks. That electric spark that had siz-
zled burst into life again, turning his preconceived
notions about her on their head. It was disturbing
and he didn't like it. He frowned and dragged his
thoughts to heel.

She was… *Was she criticising him?*

For the first time in his life, Dante found himself on the back foot with no response readily
available.

'Like I said, I respected your privacy.'

'But now you've decided to use what I said at
that interview against me.'

'Kate, what I am offering is not exactly water
torture. As my wife, you'll have a life in which

everything you could possibly need or want will
be at your disposal. In addition to that, you'll walk
away from it a young woman with the world at
her feet, able to do anything you want, no expense spared.

'Of course, a pre-nup will be necessary to avoid
the possibility of greed trumping common sense
but, that notwithstanding, you'll find me an ex-
ceptionally generous man. If you've been saving
to buy your own house, pay off debts—hell, if
you want to treat yourself to a yacht or a lifetime
of holidays on exotic islands—then you'll be able
to afford to do so! In return, I ask for two years
of your life, during which we will share space as
friends. This may not be the sort of marriage you
dreamt of but you'll have nothing but my greatest
respect for its duration.'

Kate opened her mouth to object, then she thought
of her parents. When she had sat them down and
laid bare the groundwork for the life they would
lead, the one she would do her best to subsidise,
her father had cried. She had never seen him cry
before and it had stuck in her head, a permanent
reminder of what they had gone and were still
going through, and the hardships, tough times and
pitfalls that still lay along the way.

Their place was tiny and cramped with belong-
ings they had accumulated in their many travels,
none of which they had been willing to dispose

of. The therapist steadily continued to eat away at her salary and the farming her dad had insisted on—because he couldn't envisage himself ever doing anything that wasn't to do with the land—ate money and gave very little back in return. He had to have someone to help with the heavy stuff, and the equipment was astonishing, considering the small acreage being cultivated.

But would he stop? Absolutely not. He'd given up his beloved travelling, with each day an adventure, and there was no way he was going to suffocate doing something in front of a computer indoors. He needed to be outside, to feel the air on his face and breathe in nature.

Nature and fresh air didn't come cheap, especially when he was still in the floundering stages of small-time farming. But there was no way she would do anything to deter him because his mental health was the most important thing in the world to her.

As Dante's uncle's was to him—not to mention Angelina. As he had said, her well-being would be integral to the peculiar arrangement he was suggesting. The two people in the world he cared for the most were the beating heart of this deal…

'And what happens after two years?' she heard herself ask. 'Even though,' she hastened to add, 'It's all academic.'

'We part company.'

'And your uncle will be upset all over again,' she said quietly. 'Not to mention Angelina.'

'My uncle will be in a better place, and he will finally accept that marriage and I…no longer see eye to eye.' He smiled grimly. 'And Angelina will be nearly eleven. She will be maturing and will be able to handle the eventual break-up. And, of course, you will doubtless have a bond with her and so might wish to continue to communicate and visit…provide continuity. I would never prevent you from doing that. In truth, would it be so very different from what happens in very many families when a marriage breaks down?'

He leant towards her and she could breathe him in, a woody, clean smell that filled her nostrils and made her feel a little heady. 'Will you think about it at the very least?'

'And if I say no? What happens next? Do you cast me out?'

Dante's eyebrows shot up and he burst out laughing.

'Cast you out?' He was still amused when he finally looked at her. 'That's very melodramatic, isn't it? Where do you imagine I would cast you— into the dark wilderness? On the first ship back to England with just a crust of dry bread for the journey? To the local train station with no time for you to pack your bags?'

'Very funny,' Kate muttered *sotto voce* but, when she looked at him, something inside her did a little inexplicable flip because he suddenly looked *young*, temporarily shorn of the cold self-assurance that made him so intimidating.

'Of course I won't cast you out,' he said with wry amusement. 'I have proposed something to you, something no more or less than a business deal of sorts. I did it because I care deeply about my uncle and want to make him happy. Antonio is a good man—the best. He deserves it. But...'

He shrugged and looked at her levelly. 'If it's too much for you to consider, then so be it. Naturally your job here will not be affected in any way, shape or form and this matter will never be discussed again.'

'And you'll, I guess, find someone else suitable for the—er—role?'

'No.'

'No?'

'You are really the only one who fits the bill.' He looked at her pensively. 'I would never risk any woman getting the wrong message and that would be something very easy to do. I would also never risk anyone my daughter might not get along with, and she gets along with you. The stories she tells me... Her face lights up when she talks about you. No, you are the only one who would do—for this.'

He stood up, stretched and then rubbed the back of his neck. 'My apologies for interrupting your evening...'

'Signor D'Agostino... Dante...um, I'll think

about it, about your proposal.' Their eyes collided but Kate didn't look away. 'I'm very fond of your uncle.' She smiled awkwardly. 'And the money would come in very handy. I'm just being honest.'

'I like that. As I mentioned, this would be a business proposition. We would have separate quarters, naturally, but should you accept the details would be hammered out between us and all the necessary legalities would be arranged. I have a team of extremely discreet lawyers.'

'*If* I accept…'

Dante smiled and Kate did her best to hold on to her composure because she could read triumph in that smile.

But it was a tempting proposition.

If it weren't for her dad, for the financial commitments that made it so hard for her to put aside any money for her own future, then she would never be here now, considering his outrageous proposition.

But…

The thought of giving them the sort of lifestyle that might go some way to compensating for what they had lost—maybe even a little caravan so that they could sate some of the wanderlust that would never really desert them… The thought of the freedom to do this without the cold anxiety of how far any money she earned could ever go…

Temptation dangled in front of her like a banquet spread wide to tempt a starving beggar.

Surely two years wasn't an eternity to put aside when the rewards were so tempting?

She would still be young, but she would be settled, with her parents' and her futures secure. And it wasn't as though he was asking her to do anything but share space under his roof. As he'd been keen to point out, they would have their separate quarters. She wondered if that was common anyway in his world, where the rules most people obeyed didn't seem to exist.

'I'll think about it.' She glanced away but, had he looked into her eyes, he surely would have seen capitulation.

She said yes.

Dante looked at her over the continental breakfast laid out on the table between them the following morning. With Angelina dropped off to school and all calls on hold for the next couple of hours, allowing him to discuss the details of their marriage, he seemed quietly satisfied.

'I'll arrange a meeting with my lawyers as quickly as possible,' he said in response. 'But first we have to go over the bare bones of this arrangement—make sure we're on the same page.' He nodded at the spread of breads and jams in front of them. 'And eat something, Kate. You're allowed.'

Oddly, and despite the fact that she had been working for him for over two years, this was the first time Kate had sat down and shared a meal with him without the presence of his daughter or other people around.

Kate's eyes skittered away from his but she was still very much aware of him in her peripheral vision as she reached for a croissant. He was dressed in black jeans and a heavy cream shirt rolled to the elbows with the top two buttons undone, revealing a sprinkling of dark hair. When she looked at him, she was struck by the notion that she had agreed to marry this man, a guy who sent her nervous system into freefall and with whom she had nothing in common.

'This feels strange,' she confessed.

'That's because it *is* strange. That said, I very much appreciate you agreeing to my proposal. I must ask you whether you are absolutely sure that you want to go ahead with this because, once the announcement is put out there, retracting it would be…somewhat awkward.'

'Two years isn't a long time in the grand scheme of things.'

'Especially given the financial incentive,' Dante murmured. For the first time, he found that he was intensely curious about why the money mattered so much to her. Was she saving for a fancy house in a fancy neighbourhood? Paying off a student loan and whatever debts she might have accumulated when she had been studying? Investing in gold bars—because who could ever go wrong with that?

Certainly, there was no significant other on the scene. That had been mentioned in passing only a couple of months ago, when he had had to ask her to work for three weeks over the summer holidays which she'd been due to have off to return to England.

'Of course, please tell me whether you have commitments of a personal nature, in which case I can try and arrange a fill-in from the agency until Sara is well enough to return after her operation.' He hadn't bothered to beat about the bush.

Sara, the middle-aged woman who covered the holiday period with Angelina, had been rushed to hospital with appendicitis.

'Personal nature?'

'A boyfriend, perhaps?'

He had shrugged away the potential intrusiveness of the question but his dark eyes had been watchful.

'I—no… I'm a free agent, as it happens…'

At the time, Kate had struggled not to laugh—boyfriend? She had spent most of her life living in and out of suitcases with her parents. Certainly, during her teenage years, when most girls her age had been navigating their way through the complex world of boys and first relationships, she had been busy making sure she kept abreast with schoolwork. With her in and out of various schools, there had simply never been the opportunity to build any kind of relationship with any boy. Then, just when she had found stability, settling into her career, the unexpected had happened with her father's accident to sweep her back off her feet. Boys were a luxury she had just never got round to sampling.

'We'll have to work out a timetable to break the news, but I suggest telling Antonio first and then waiting for him to digest it.'

'He's going to be a little surprised.'

'As understatements go, you could very well be right.'

'Is he actually going to believe that we're a couple?'

'People are always keen to believe what they want to believe. At any rate, looked at logically, it would make a lot more sense than were I to produce a brand-new fiancée from nowhere, like a magician pulling a rabbit from a hat. But the truth is, my uncle knows you and likes you, and I doubt he's going to question our arrangement when he's made such a fuss of marrying me off.'

He flushed and then confessed, with just a trace of discomfort, 'I'm not sure he would be thrilled and impressed were I to show up with one of the women I usually date dangling on my arm with a diamond on her finger, anyway... He's met two of my past girlfriends and has been noisy in his disapproval.'

Kate's lips twitched. 'Noisy in his disapproval?'

'You'd be surprised,' Dante said drily, 'How much can be conveyed through a series of snorts, eye rolling, sighing heavily and head shaking.'

Kate threw her head back and laughed, a proper belly laugh that surprised her, because since when had Dante D'Agostino been the sort who encouraged hoots of laughter?

'What sort of women have you dated in the past?' The directness of the question surprised her as much as her laughter just had, and she saw him hesitate. But, more daringly, she added, 'If we're supposed to be a couple, then surely we'll need to know a few things about one another?' She blushed and ducked her gaze, dipping her finger into some of the crumbs on her plate and licking them off without looking at him. 'I only ask because I can't remember you ever...'

'I never have. I've always refused to allow Angelina to be witness to my love life. I...may not see my daughter as much as I know I should, but every decision taken has her at the very centre of it.'

Kate nodded approvingly and he continued in the voice of someone making a decision, but a decision that might not have come easily,

'Unchallenging,' he said. 'My girlfriends—fun, unchallenging...beautiful.'

Kate smiled and nodded, and wished she hadn't asked the question, because of course those were the sort of women this man would be attracted to. His wife had been shockingly beautiful and it was unlikely he would have strayed far from that benchmark.

'I'm guessing my uncle will have the champagne on tap when I break the news to him that you're going to be my wife,' Dante murmured with wry amusement.

'I expect he will.' Her smile felt stiff and painful. If his uncle had snorted with horror at a parade of sexy, unchallenging beauties, then of course he would approve of the dowdy nanny who looked after his beloved great-niece.

'But, before we say a word, I think it might be appropriate that he perhaps sees you in a slightly different light. He might have his own doubts about the speed with which I've suddenly become attached to you, but he can be persuaded into believing that I've simply woken up to the potential of someone who isn't quite what he thinks. He may very well like to imagine that what might have been an already existing loose relationship between us has crystallised into something more, thanks to his prompting.'

'What do you mean?'

'My uncle lives some distance away from my place in Milan,' Dante mused thoughtfully. 'It's fair to say that that lends itself to a romance happening behind the scenes, one of which he would be ignorant. That said…'

He looked at her carefully, handsome head tilted to one side, his stare unwavering until she had to control the urge to squirm.

'That said…?' she prompted, to move the conversation along.

He flushed and for the first time looked truly uncomfortable.

'Look, I wouldn't want you to take this the wrong way…'

'Take what the wrong way?' Kate asked, instantly suspicious.

'Eh, in keeping with your new role, it might be prudent… How do I put this…?'

'What? If you have something to say, then might I suggest that you just say it?'

She narrowed her eyes, pursed her lips and was undeterred when he said, 'Is this the stern-teacher face you pull out of the box when my back is turned?'

She folded her arms and waited and, grudgingly, he murmured, 'The small matter of your wardrobe.'

'What about my wardrobe?'

The lingering silence spoke volumes. He was allowing her to join the dots, and join the dots she did.

Her choice of clothing just wasn't going to cut it. Kate gritted her teeth together and did her best not to take it as a personal insult. She told herself that it was no more insulting than applying for any job that required a specific uniform. She had accepted an unusual job and she would be required to have a specific uniform.

'I see…'

'You find my remark offensive.'

'No, of course not. Why should I?'

'You want to say something. Say it. We're on a different footing now.' He relaxed back and stretched out his long legs to one side, crossing them at the ankles. His expression was cool and questioning, and that made her bristle. He was so composed, so assured, so controlled and basically so unperturbed by something that might not have been meant as a barb but had wounded like one.

If they were to embark on this different footing, then maybe it would be a good time to lay down her own ground rules or else risk getting lost without a voice, agreeing to every condition laid down whether she wanted to or not.

'Fine. I get it,' she said curtly. 'If I am to play a convincing part, then it's important that I play the part well. And, sure, if I show up on your arm and I'm no longer the dowdy nanny he's accustomed to, he might get it into his head that perhaps the whole "overnight marriage" thing isn't quite as preposterous as it seems… But please don't think that you can give orders and expect instant obedience, *Dante*. How would you feel if *I* asked *you* to change elements of *your* wardrobe?'

'What elements?'

'Your…your shirts,' she said, waving vaguely at him and scowling. 'Maybe I don't really like shirts with monograms on the pockets. Maybe I find them stuffy.'

'Do you?'

'Possibly.' She was suddenly horrified at this change of role and disoriented by the speed with which everything was suddenly happening.

'What else?'

'I don't have a list at my disposal. I just want…' She sighed, 'I just want…'

'You won't be.'

'You don't know what I'm going to say.'

'You don't want to think that you're jumping into a fast-flowing current with no control over any riptides underneath that might drag you away.'

'How did you know?'

'My apologies for offending you by suggesting a rethink on your wardrobe. If you really want to stick with what you have, then of course I'm not going to force you into a shopping spree. But, aside from the business of enticing my uncle into believing our piece of fiction, there will be functions and galas you'll be required to attend…'

He grimaced and smiled. 'As few as humanly possible, if I have anything to do with it, but that aside there will undoubtedly be numerous occasions that call for...dressier outfits than you probably have. You might find that it's just a lot more comfortable if you choose to blend in by wearing them.

'And then my uncle... He might be a little sceptical, if I'm to be completely honest. It would certainly mark a seismic change for me to be suddenly seriously involved with a woman who can't relax in my company and shows up dressed for a day at the office when we go out together.' He grinned. 'And if, in return, you want me to put my monogrammed shirts into storage for the duration of our marriage, then consider it done.'

'I don't care about the shirts,' she said truthfully. 'Like you said, what I do care about is an arrangement where I feel I've relinquished control.'

'Trust me.' He leaned forward and his dark eyes were urgent and serious. 'This is a pact, and we each hold one half of the steering wheel. We'll adjust to move around one another in harmony. I would never ask you to do anything you wouldn't want to do. Of course, should you wish to have an...arrangement...with someone, then discretion would be imperative...'

Dante lowered his eyes and his thoughts flew with unerring speed to a scenario that made his senses stir. This woman, naked on a bed, her clothes discarded, wearing only a small, slow half-smile, beckoning with the promise of sexual gratification. He felt sudden heat pour through him and gritted his teeth in exasperation.

'When I have an arrangement with someone—by which I guess you mean find a guy—then I won't be in a different kind of arrangement with someone else. When I choose to have a relationship with someone, then I will do so as a free person so I can have a meaningful relationship that's actually going somewhere. Two years isn't exactly a lifetime to wait.'

'Have you ever had one of those meaningful relationships as a free person before?' Dante asked with genuine curiosity, and Kate blushed and stammered.

'I'm still young. I've…been busy forging a career and of course, being over here, working…'

'You know there were never restrictions imposed on how you spent your free time here,' he returned quietly with some consternation, and she smiled shyly.

'I know.' She wondered what he would have made of her life lived on the move. Of her parents, happy to globe-trot with her in tow. In many ways, he'd been right when he said that she would be good in this role, because they were so very different that there would never be any chance of either of them being confused into thinking that what they had might be more than it was.

Two people from different planets could never

forge bonds that were anything but superficial. She relaxed and smiled with real warmth. They *would* move round one another in harmony, and it was fantastic of him to suggest that she keep in touch with Angelina when it was all over—as she would with Antonio, no doubt.

And, in the meantime, a frightened old man would feel calm and content and able to deal with what the immediate future might have in store for him.

This would work, and the thought of not having to shoulder a future of potential financial problems, of her parents being happy and her father's mental health getting back to where it once used to be, filled her with sudden, soaring euphoria.

'I'm happy to have the Cinderella makeover,' she said with a tentative smile. 'Now that the pumpkin is going to become a carriage, and the dress code for a carriage is completely different...'

'Good! As long as you realise that I'll never be your Prince Charming...'

Kate's smile widened and she laughed.

'I think it's safe to say that you could never be my Prince Charming and, while I'm married to you, I won't be looking for one either. As for you...' She shrugged and, for a few heart-stopping seconds, their eyes met and held and the breath left her in a sudden, inexplicable whoosh.

But when she blinked that unsettling feeling was gone and her voice was amused and neutral.

'You're free to do as you please, and I know you'll be discreet.'

'Well.' He raised his cup of coffee to her. 'Here's to the perfect arrangement. Tomorrow, we can take step one…'

CHAPTER THREE

STEP ONE, in actual fact, came several days later when Dante informed her that they would be going to meet Antonio, staying there a couple of days.

In that time, life had moved at warp speed. Documents had been signed. Kate's hand had hovered over the final page, and she had reminded herself that this was simply a two-year contract during which she would still have duties, but of a different kind.

Although, in actual fact, her time with Angelina would remain the same. She had insisted on that. She might assume the mantle of wife, but she had no intention of assuming a change of lifestyle to the extent that she packed in the thing she loved doing and replaced it with the sort of thing she imagined wives and partners of very rich men did: shopped; lunched; spent crazy amounts of time having bits of their bodies tinkered with…

When she had explained that to Dante, he had burst out laughing and told her that she could do as she liked. Indeed, he'd said, he liked the idea that there would be continuity with his daughter, that she wouldn't have to endure the inconvenience of having a replacement nanny foisted onto her.

Kate had taken that to mean the less disruption to his daily routine, the better. She would also have ample time off to go and see her parents. That had been something else upon which she had insisted without going into any details about why it was so important to her.

'As you wish.' Dante had shrugged and she'd gathered that, when it came to the lives of rich, powerful, Italian nobility, evenings of bonding around the telly and walks together at the weekend throwing sticks for the dogs weren't things that were particularly valued. Or maybe they weren't of value *to him*. He had not batted an eyelid at the prospect of her being away from a couple of weeks at a time. She expected his ex-wife was the one he had cherished and, when she had died, so had the importance of the family values she had always taken as a given.

Things were in place. And so was her new, improved wardrobe. She had been handed several credit cards and instructed to spend as much as she wanted, wherever she wanted.

'I could accompany you,' he had said, glancing up from his computer as she had stood in front of the massive desk in the suite of rooms he occasionally used as his offices, when he wanted uninterrupted time to work. 'If you feel you may need input.'

Horrified by the thought of having Dante traipse from boutique to boutique with her, giving his verdict on the clothes she would be wearing, she'd shaken her head vigorously and told him that she was perfectly capable of doing a little clothes shopping on her own. It wasn't rocket science. She would take Angelina with her, which had made him smile—a smile that knocked years off him.

There would be a shared diary of events, updated by email daily so that she would know what was planned from one week to the next.

'Although,' he had told her, 'Most of my time will be spent working. If there are any invitations you feel a particular interest in attending, then naturally I'd be more than happy to oblige. But, like I said, I try and avoid those meet-and-greet social affairs.'

'Why?' Kate had asked and the look he'd thrown her had been part-surprise, part-disapproval.

Had she breached a boundary line? She was getting the feeling that he had a great deal of those in place, but he had said noncommittally, 'I usually can't quite see the point of them. I'm generous in my charity donations, so fundraising galas are an unnecessary indulgence, and if I want to mix with the elite, I can do so in my own time and at my own convenience.'

End of conversation.

Angelina had no idea that anything was remiss although, as Kate now paused to glance at her reflection in the floor-to-ceiling mirror in her sitting room, she could see the eight-year-old gazing at her with some surprise. They had had their shopping expedition, with Kate tactfully avoiding most of her little charge's outlandish suggestions of fur and sequins. Afterwards, Dante had unexpectedly surprised them both by taking his daughter off for some tea, a gesture which had been greeted with breathless excitement and yelps of pleasure.

But had she extrapolated anything from that shopping trip? Judging from the surprised expression on her face now, Kate wryly thought maybe not.

The casual, non-working uniform of jeans and a jumper had been replaced by pale-grey cashmere culottes, a grey cashmere jumper and some flat, black ankle boots. The outfit had cost the earth. The soft black coat which would accompany the outfit had also been eye-wateringly expensive. Her initial hesitation about buying stuff she would never have dreamt of buying, because frugality was part and parcel of her DNA, had been firmly squashed by reminding herself that *this was a job.*

Dante was as remote as he had been before, and would remain that way. It would be up to her to play the game as coolly as he did. He would be irritated if she made a big deal every time she bought anything new, because money was no object to him and so henceforth should be no object to her. Indeed, she suspected that her off-the-peg clothes and second-hand vintage stuff she found in charity shops would have filled him with quiet horror and embarrassment, had she paraded them in front of his exclusive friends and family.

'We're going to see stay with your Uncle Antonio for a few days.'

'Is that some of the stuff we bought?'

'Er…yes.'

'You look pretty.'

'Thank you.' She caught Angelina's gaze in the mirror and smiled. 'Not too much grey?'

'I have that nice yellow and red scarf you could borrow.'

'If it's the one I'm thinking of, with the sequins and the sparkles and the ponies, then I'll say no.' She grinned. 'Much more suited to you than to me, I think.' She hesitated, then said in a rush, 'And your dad is going to be there as well.'

'Is he?'

Angelina, who had been sprawled on one of the chairs playing games on her tablet, sat up, alert and bristling with excitement.

'You never said! Naughty!'

'He only confirmed the timings last night. Are you pleased?'

'How long is he going to be there?'

'I'm not sure, darling. Hopefully, the whole time…' She felt the familiar tug on her heartstrings at Angelina's breathless, childish thrill at the thought of having her dad around for several days on end. He was so busy—he lived life in the fast lane, with time spent with his daughter precious and erratic, although in fairness, when he *was* with her, he was one hundred percent *with* her.

She watched as Angelina leapt off the chair and danced around the room for a couple of minutes.

She was a beautiful child with very, very long dark hair, soulful dark eyes and her father's smooth, olive complexion. Serious most of the time, when she laughed her face lit up, and she was laughing now. In that moment, a streak of rebelliousness shot through Kate like an injection of adrenaline.

It would be easy to fall into a routine of fading into the background, but she had made a start laying down her own rules, and she wasn't going to allow him to nod and agree and then proceed to do exactly as he wanted.

He was that kind of guy, from everything she had seen over time. He lived a charmed life surrounded by people who did as he told them to. She had never met his parents, but hanging in one of the many formal living areas was an imposing oil painting of them together and they looked formidable, as formidable as their only son.

In this mutually beneficial arrangement, however, he was no more in charge of her than she was of him and gut instinct told her that it was important to remember that.

His chauffeur would drive them from Milan to the outskirts of Venice, where Dante was already with his uncle. The next few hours were spent packing and then travelling in the luxury of Dante's car, one of his fleet of cars, and the least sporty but the most comfortable.

It was a shame they couldn't detour to see Lake Como or explore Verona, with its Roman amphitheatre. Kate had only ever read about Verona when she had had her head buried in Shakespeare's *Romeo and Juliet* and had been intrigued by the romance of a city she'd never previously heard of.

It was cold and dark, and the shadowy landscape that flashed by as the car ate up the miles only hinted at the splendid beauty of hills, valleys and the sprawling vineyards that produced the Prosecco for which the region was so famed.

Kate gazed out, her mind half on the retreating dark shapes of hills and mountains standing guard around the swirling dunes of the perfectly aligned vineyards. In summer the sight would be magnificent, a sea of green interrupted by glorious clutches of houses and churches, each small town worth seeing in its own right.

Nerves were kicking in. Next to her, Angelina was slumped, asleep. As plans went, this one made sense, and the end result would be worth every second. But, as Antonio's mansion drew closer, she wondered how easy it would be to co-exist with Dante who was so cold, so intimidating, with those flashes of warmth and humanity so few and far between.

It was one thing laying down laws. It was another having the will power to follow through.

She had mentioned nothing to her parents and was toying with the idea of keeping it all under wraps. Her parents would be appalled and disappointed at anything that smacked of an arranged marriage. They had never spent a day apart, except for when her father had been in hospital. So what would be the point in breaking their hearts? She would be able to return to see them, perhaps not for entire weeks at a time, but certainly frequently. She could easily talk about loans, bonuses and her employer's generosity when it came to justifying the sums of money she would be spending on them.

Honestly, they were both naïve when it came to anything financial. Why else had they ended up as they had? The small deception would be simple enough to achieve. Only the discomfort of knowing that she was lying to them, or at the very least being incredibly economical with the truth, gave her pause for thought.

It was after eight by the time they finally made it to Antonio's palace, a frothy, wintry, extravagant concoction nestled in huge grounds and woodland. Half of it was lit like a Christmas tree, the other half in darkness. Antonio only used part of his grand house.

The car slowed as they eased up the tree-lined avenue and circled the courtyard before slowing to a stop. Before they could all emerge, the front door was open and Antonio was briefly silhouetted, before being quickly ushered inside by Dante, who towered over his uncle. Kate tensed, roused Angelina and was thankful for the distraction of her excitable chattering as they hurried inside and the front door closed against the bracing wintry weather outside.

And then the gravity of the road she was about to go down hit her. Antonio stooped to embrace Angelina; Dante looked at her with those dark, deep, cool eyes as he reached down to swing his daughter up into a bear hug. The overwhelming grandeur of the palace, with its pale marble floors and intricately sculpted ceilings, spoke to a life lived in a different world.

She wasn't just going to be playing a part for a limited period of time. She was going to be entering the world of one of Italy's most exalted families, moving amongst people she would otherwise never have met in a million years, and she was going to have to do it with credibility.

How on earth was that going to work out?

Apprehension and excitement hit her in equal measure. As she stepped towards Dante, she felt a momentary keening towards him as the one solid point in a world that had suddenly been turned on its head and, as though reading her mind, he steadied her, placing his arm around her shoulders.

'Are you all right?' he murmured, voice low as Antonio, still stooping, engaged with a suddenly lively Angelina.

'It's been a long day...'

'Of course.' He drew back and began ushering them towards the kitchen, while giving orders for the bags to be taken up to their respective quarters.

She looked amazing. How had he failed to pay attention to the clear-eyed beauty shyly hiding behind her dutiful subservience? There was nothing obvious about her but, dressed in that casually elegant outfit, she was somehow so intensely alluring that he was shocked at his own reaction. He didn't want to be sabotaged by his body, and had no intention of allowing that to happen, but he was still disconcerted enough to remove himself and put some distance between them.

'I should take Angelina up,' Kate offered. 'Is it the usual room?'

But she hesitated when Angelina stopped, folded her arms and demanded her dad do the bedtime routine. His being around for a bedtime ritual was rare, and it was only when she glanced across to see Antonio looking shrewdly at this sketch that she blushed, not quite knowing what to do. Did she tear Angelina away from her father, politely insist? Remind Dante what he was supposed to do when presented with his daughter's current book?

'Dante, I think your daughter demands that you settle her.' Antonio chuckled, removing the decision from her hands. His eyes were sharp. 'Kate, why not sit with me a while? It has been some time since we chatted.'

Kate met Dante's dark gaze and their eyes tangled and held for a few breathless seconds. Yes, Dante might have an idea of his daughter's bedtime ritual, but he was so very often back late. Bedtime rituals with young children were always evolving, sometimes on the back of something as small as what might have happened at school that day, some childish gossip far more important than whatever book happened to be on the go.

Kate lowered her eyes but her lips twitched, and she knew that Dante was very much aware of the sudden flash of amusement on her face, just as he knew exactly what she was thinking.

She turned to Antonio and smiled brightly, and was aware of Dante hovering uncertainly as they both left him to his own devices and headed towards the kitchen. She could hear Angelina's excited chatter fading in the background.

'No staff,' Antonio said, settling her and then fetching them both a glass of wine. 'Food has been prepared and is in the oven. Supper when Dante is back down. You may have noticed that much of the palace has been closed off. I confine myself to a few rooms. It is my health and my age. It is all too much. But what joy to have you all here, and let us not mention how heart-warming and unusual to see my nephew fulfilling his paternal duties...'

'Unusual?'

'As unusual as you all being here, visiting the invalid at the same time, my dear.'

'You're hardly an invalid,' Kate teased gently, although she could see lines of anxiety etched on his face that she couldn't recall being there before. Had Dante mentioned anything? They should have spoken, but too late now.

'That is very kind of you, my dear. But enough of me. It is good to have you all under my roof for the first time.'

'Hardly for the first time...'

'Ah, but not often enough, my dear. An old man comes to rely on these small pleasures. Seeing you together... I should take this opportunity to tell you a little of my beloved nephew, although I should also add that this is to remain between the two of us.'

'I—I'm not sure I want to be in a position, er…'

'In a position of hearing about my nephew? Now, now. At heart, are we all not curious about one another?'

Kate burst out laughing and Antonio smiled broadly.

'That's below the belt.' She was still laughing when she said that.

'But is it not the truth?' He gestured broadly, briefly reminding her of Dante, who often made the same exotic, expansive gestures when he talked. 'He is a product of his background. A harsh upbringing, my dear, will always breed a man who is unfamiliar with the gentler side of human nature.'

This was the first time Antonio had ever delved into any kind of personal commentary on his nephew. They had always got along famously. He adored Angelina, and was fun to be around, but confidences of this nature? Never in the past.

Something trickled through her but she couldn't pin it down. She was suddenly eaten up with curiosity. It swept through her like a tidal wave, making her wonder how long it had been there, like a pernicious weed waiting for an opportunity to push through the polite barriers she had always had in place–a month? Six months? A year? Ever since the first moment she had seen him and been rendered mute by the shock of his dark, dangerous beauty and his cold but stupidly charismatic remoteness?

That, too, sent a trickle of *something* through her.

'He's an incredibly kind man,' she heard herself say, meaning every word of it. 'And very fair. A *good* man.'

Antonio's bushy eyebrows shot up but he smiled and nodded approvingly. 'He is all those things and more—but his parents? My brother? They were strict, cold, did not believe in displays of emotion. Dante was reared to inherit the crown, so to speak. He was never allowed the little freedoms his friends enjoyed.'

Kate listened in silence but she felt the sting of sympathy prick the back of her eyes.

She could all too well picture a boy developing into a man, his life conditioned to point in one direction, with the weight of his future duties resting heavily on his shoulders.

She knew what Antonio was telling her. He was telling her that there was a reason his nephew was so stilted with his daughter, and she was suddenly desperate to dig deeper, to find out if he had always been like that even when he had been married. Had he relied on his first wife to provide the things his upbringing had not equipped him to provide, such as spontaneity and a sense of play-fulness? The ease of a physical connection?

She also wanted to ask him what had prompted his sudden urge to confide but, before she could work out how to broach that delicate subject, he leaned into her and confided, 'Old I may be, my dear, but far from an old fool. Not long ago, I told my nephew that it was time for him to leave the past behind, to marry, and now...' he sat back and spread his arms wide with a satisfied expression '...here you are. Both of you! What a happy oc-currence!'

What had they done? Kate thought. Was he suspicious? Or did he think that she and Dante were—*what?* A happy couple in love? In some place of blissful courtship which had been sim-mering for months on the sly? Dante must have let something slip, given some hint of what was to come. This was all part of their arrangement, discussed in advance, and yet deceit carried its own rancid odour.

In that moment, she decided that she would spare her parents that deceit. In the meantime, she opened her mouth at least to try and quell some of his unrealistic expectations but, before she could say a word, the kitchen door was pushed open and Dante was with them.

She drew in a sharp breath, aware of him as never before and wondering whether it was be-cause of what Antonio had told her.

'Dante…' She caught his eye and tried to signal something but he raised his eyebrows, smiled and told her that he had found it impossible to follow the plot in the ballerina book Angelina had insisted he read to her.

'You might want to make a habit of it,' Kate quipped, the sudden tension draining out of her, because he looked hassled but rather pleased with himself. Maybe also because he had assumed a three-dimensional aspect that he had been so determined to conceal, at least from her, a history that somehow pushed through all her preconceived notions of him. 'You'll soon realise that Daisy's unrealistic adventures are as nothing compared to some of the other classics she enjoys reading. Monty the Rat will leave you puzzled for many days.'

He flashed her a sudden smile that knocked her sideways and she blinked in confusion.

'Now, children…' Antonio clapped his hands, summoning them to order and snapping Kate out of her temporary feeling of dislocation.

'Is champagne called for?'

'Your uncle…' Kate cleared her throat. 'Has… er…'

'Pre-empted our announcement? I would have broken the news to you myself, Antonio, but I thought it best to wait until Kate got here with Angelina.' Dante smoothly relieved her of her stuttering attempt to steer the conversation.

'I expect Dante told you, my dear, about my health situation?'

'He did, Antonio, and honestly—I'm sure you're getting worked up over something that will be manageable. Times have moved on hugely when it comes to treatment for various cancers.'

'I prefer not to rely on the possibility of good fortune, my dear. There is nothing worse than misplaced optimism. I had no idea, when I expressed my desire that Dante marry, that you and he were, how should I put this, perhaps already an item?'

'We…we…er…'

'The tentative beginnings,' Dante said smoothly. 'No shouting from the rooftops, naturally, but as you know that isn't my style anyway.' He smiled at Kate, inviting her to step into the story he was spinning. 'But perhaps you hastened things…'

'Well, I cannot apologise for that, Dante.'

'You must be a little surprised,' Kate ventured as she felt the brush of Dante's arm against hers.

'I am too old for surprises and too close to meeting my maker to question them when they come. Now, let us enjoy the moment for what it is. A time to celebrate! The finest champagne is called for.'

'I take it there is no shortage in the fridge?'

'Ah, Dante, how well you know me…what is a man without champagne?'

He moved away from her, strolling towards Antonio. There had been no display of pseudo-affection. As he'd said, not his style.

It wouldn't be expected. Dante wasn't a guy who did public displays of affection, and for him to change tack would be astonishing. That hit her in a flash. This would truly be nothing more than a business arrangement and, although that should have lifted her spirits, she felt a twinge of disappointment.

Was it because, with Antonio's unexpected confidence, a box had been opened? Were opened boxes ever a good thing? Didn't they usually herald unpleasant surprises?

She had grown accustomed to the travelling life she had led with her parents. But she could remember a time when she had been very young— maybe Angelina's age—when her parents would sit her down, look at one another with barely contained excitement…and she would know, with a sinking feeling, that everything was about to change once again.

Time to move on. There'd be some weeks or months building up friendships, but then would come the call of the unknown, and the suitcases and boxes would be packed and onward bound they would go… While she had looked back through the window of whatever old car they had been driving at another disappearing view of what might have been.

Opened boxes weren't for her. She knew that she would do well to remember that.

Champagne was popped and she smiled until her jaw ached. Overjoyed, Antonio was unquestioning when it came to the details of their sudden romance. Dante tossed some vague crumbs out there and Antonio accepted them and moved on. Perhaps he preferred mystery over chapter and verse, or perhaps he was just relieved that his nephew was going to marry and settle down.

She allowed her eyes to wander to the man she would marry and she shivered. Her gaze drifted from the harsh, chiselled perfection of his aristocratic features to the brown column of his neck and the latent strength of his broad shoulders.

And then it drifted further down as she half-listened to them both talking about some of the various strands of the D'Agostino empire that would require Dante's input in preparation for his uncle fully retreating from all business concerns. This was the business end of their marriage, she thought: the way wealthy, powerful families operated. Giggly wedding planning wasn't for them.

Antonio began flagging shortly after dinner was eaten. He waved aside Kate's offer to tidy up. Staff would be back first thing and would be dismayed to find their job done for them.

Dante offered to accompany him to his quarters but was likewise waved away, and within minutes, he and Kate found themselves alone in the kitchen with the empty bottle of champagne on the table.

With a sharp tug of embarrassment, Kate banished from her head all wayward thoughts of the breath-taking physicality of Dante.

'I would say that went smoother than expected.' Dante raked his fingers through his hair and slanted her a glance. 'Of course, he started fishing as soon as I got here. The fact that we were both going to be here for no particular occasion had his antennae bristling. You've been shopping, I see.'

Kate blushed and nodded, and felt awkward as Dante's dark gaze rested briefly on her. 'You *did* suggest it...'

'Suits you,' he murmured. 'Subtle but elegant.' Yes, it was the first thing he had noticed when she and Angelina had hurried in, because it was the first time he'd seen her in anything other than the sort of background gear she seemed so fond of wearing.

But had he intended to say anything? He just hadn't been able to help himself in the face of her elegance...the slight gracefulness of her body... She might not have the careless, flamboyant confidence of a lot of the women he'd known, including his ex-wife, but there was a certain understated elegance about her that was equally *sexy.* More so, if anything. He dropped his gaze and felt his breathing quicken.

Kate fiddled nervously with the stem of her wine glass and sneaked a glance at Dante from under her lashes.

A white loose shirt emphasised the burnished tone of his skin and she was fascinated by the whorls of hair curling around the dull chrome metal band of his watch.

From this angle, she was offered a tantalising glimpse of muscular thighs spread apart encased in casual dark trousers that managed to look coolly elegant and wildly sexy at the same time.

Why was her focus suddenly drifting—because he'd made some offhand remark about the clothes she happened to be wearing?

'I'm surprised he wasn't more inquisitive,' she said, reverting to safer waters. 'But I suppose that's all for the good. One thing we haven't discussed is the actual business of the wedding. I realise you're a very important person over here and—'

'No need to worry on that score,' Dante interrupted. When she arched her eyebrows, he continued neutrally, 'I had the big deal when I married Angelina's mother. I have no intention of a repeat performance, whatever happens to be expected of me.'

'Oh. Good.'

'Any other questions or concerns?'

'I—I felt awful about deceiving your uncle,'

she said quietly. 'I know this is a done deal, but I suppose being here…watching his face light up…'

Dante tilted his head to one side and gazed at her in silence for such a long time that she began to fidget.

'You're very sentimental, aren't you?'

'I—I've never really thought about it, to be honest.'

'When you're with Angelina, when you talk about her, your face is transformed and the same just then—you looked damp-eyed, imagining that we are in the process of committing a heinous crime by entering into this contract.'

Kate shrugged. 'I—I don't think I'm out of the ordinary in feeling a twinge of guilt. It's just that you—you're—'

'What? What am I?'

'I wouldn't want to offend you.'

'I wouldn't worry on that score,' Dante said gently. 'I don't offend easily.'

'Well, then, I guess you're so…*cold*. Do you ever really *laugh*? Have you ever let your hair down?' She shot him a helpless look from under her lashes. 'You—you're like a robot!' She instantly wished she could take those hurtful words back as a dark flush delineated his sharp cheekbones.

'I'm sorry,' she said in a rush.

'Why?' He shrugged. 'We're just very different people.'

'And, yet when you came back into the kitchen, I could see you really enjoyed that bedtime ritual with Angelina.'

Dante shifted and went to pour himself some more champagne, only to discover that they had finished the bottle, so drank some water instead. His flush deepened and he glanced at her.

'I… It was, yes… I enjoyed it. Doesn't happen often. My fault. I should…' He raked his fingers through his hair and frowned. He could hear the stiffness in his voice but knew he couldn't fight it. It was just who he was, for better or for worse, and yet, next to her open, transparent spontaneity, that stiffness made him feel a thousand years old.

'Should what?'

'Nothing. It is… Life's far too short for regrets.'

'But never too short for new beginnings,' Kate returned gently. 'We're here tomorrow. Why don't you take Angelina somewhere—out for the day? Not just an expensive meal somewhere.'

'I…'

'Is that a yes?'

'Yes,' he said, voice low. He shot her a look from under thick, sooty lashes. 'But…perhaps you would agree to come with us both…?'

'It's a deal.' She smiled and her heart fluttered when he slowly smiled back.

CHAPTER FOUR

OF COURSE THEY must go—and not to the local town! Venice and no less would do!

Antonio practically ushered them to the front door the following morning when Kate tentatively mooted the idea, making sure to dilute it with lots of apologies for leaving him, but he was having none of it.

'This old man has no intention of standing in the way of two lovebirds!' He had winked at them both while Angelina had been busy weighing up various breakfast options, all home-baked and spread on the vast marble-topped ten-seater which limply tried to pass itself off as a casual kitchen table. 'And no need to hurry back!' he had boomed, a far cry from the pallid, uncertain man of a day ago. 'I have things lined up.'

'Things?' Dante, in the middle helping himself to a bread roll and filling it with cheese, moved as he ate and half-peered at his laptop, which was open and blinking with emails. 'What things?'

Antonio huffed with a flush. 'As it happens, I

remember I have an appointment with the consultant this morning.'

'What?' Dante slammed shut his computer, glanced at his watch and then at his uncle. 'Time?'

'I am not following you.' Antonio busied himself with breakfast, making a deal out of pouring himself some coffee and stirring sugar into it while avoiding eye contact with Dante.

'Time of your appointment?'

'You will be in Venice! Beautiful winter weather out there, and a lovely time of year to visit—fewer crowds! Did you know that there are over three hundred bridges in Venice? Staggering!'

Dante caught Kate's eye and she raised her eyebrows sympathetically.

'I feel it might be impossible to be in two places at once, Antonio.'

'If that is your way of telling me that I am not capable of making my way to see a doctor without having my hand held, son, then I will try not to take offence!'

'Antonio…!'

'Angelina, why don't we go and get changed to go out…?' This from Kate, who was vaguely wondering how it was that she and Dante had managed to morph into *love birds* when the picture they'd so far presented was of two people who barely knew one another and certainly weren't keeling over with loving looks.

'Stay!' Dante swung to look at her, adding in a gentler voice, that was nevertheless still thick with frustration, 'Please.' He looked at Angelina and smiled tersely. 'Angelina, perhaps you might go to your room and, eh, get ready, as Kate has suggested? We will be with you in a matter of minutes.'

Accustomed to doing as she was told, Angelina didn't utter a word of protest. She immediately headed to the door. For a few seconds Kate found it hard to recall that look on Dante's face the evening before, when there had been something there, something warm and a little uncertain, but quietly happy after he had settled his daughter. This was now the face of the distant father she was accustomed to. The man who had been raised to be as cold and remote as his own parents had been, as Antonio had explained.

Instead of pulling back, though, Kate had to bank down a peculiar surge of warmth and empathy towards this harsh, complex man who was suddenly fleshing out into a three-dimensional guy as compelling as he was good-looking. She didn't want or need *compelling*, however.

She slowly turned to look at them both as the door quietly closed behind Angelina. She sat at the table so that now she and Antonio were both sitting, while Dante stood towering above them. He radiated power and intent while Antonio bristled with pious self-defence.

'Do you really think I would let you face those demons on your own, Antonio?' Dante asked quietly, relenting sufficiently to pull up one of the chairs, which made him no less forbidding in Kate's opinion. 'You were frightened half to death when you summoned me here to tell me the news of your diagnosis. You were still frightened even after I'd spoken to your consultant myself, and tried to relay to you the optimism which you should have been feeling. And yet you sit here and tell me that it's somehow now offensive for me to insist on coming with you to your appointment?'

'Indeed I do!' Antonio countered robustly, which Kate personally found impressive.

'Indeed *you do*?'

'I had a little blip.' Antonio lifted his shoulders with elegant dismissal, although his eyes were a little shifty when he looked away after a couple of seconds. 'We all do. Tell me you have never had the occasional little blip in your life, Dante! I appreciate everything you have done, and…'

He half-smiled and shot Kate a sly, sideways glance. 'Perhaps the glad tidings of your marriage plans have fortified me.' He beamed, reaching across to pat Dante on the arm. 'Yes, indeed, I feel I have put my finger on it! I am a new man, son. A new man with renewed purpose, and one who would very much like to face down my own demons without anyone by my side giving me advice on how to do it!'

Dante flung himself back in the chair, raked his fingers through his hair and looked utterly bewildered for a few seconds.

Kate, watching him, was tempted to smile.

He had been deprived of doing the one thing he so badly wanted to do, which was to see his uncle through troubling times, and yet she knew from her own experience that everyone had to grope their way forward on their own terms.

'If you're sure, Antonio...'

Stepping in to fill the awkward, stretching silence, Kate smiled reassuringly, and Antonio visibly relaxed, although there was something still there, something ever so slightly *guilty* in his expression. She was probably way off target with that.

'Happy you understand an old man!' He rose to his feet and shuffled to the fridge to peer inside for a few seconds, before turning to look at them. 'You young things need to get out of this stuffy house and have some fun in the City of Canals!'

Stuffy house? The kitchen was big enough to fit in most of the places where she had ever lived when she and her parents had been on the road! But he was shooing them off and, with barely any words exchanged, they were at the front door half an hour later, ready for their day of sightseeing to commence.

Angelina, on cue, had unerringly known when to reappear. This time Dante took time to look down at his daughter and then, in a gesture so rarely seen, he stooped, tenderly stroked back her hair and smiled. For a few heart-stopping seconds, Kate's breath caught in her throat and she had the awkward feeling of being witness to an intensely personal moment.

Angelina smiled at Dante, a wise, young smile, and then he scooped her up and really hugged her tight. She riffled his hair right back before he put her back down.

'It'll be fun.' He turned to Kate and smiled. 'We've been effectively dismissed by a stubborn old man, so let's get out there and do some sight-seeing.'

It took a couple of seconds to focus. She had been transported for a moment and seen the loving dad behind the stern man, but she blinked and gathered herself sufficiently to nod.

She had only managed to get to Venice a couple of times since she had started working for Dante. A combination of distance, responsibilities keeping her close to Milan and holidays back to the UK to visit her parents had clipped her wings when it came to exploring.

Then there had always been the question of money. It had never felt right to treat herself to anything frivolous when she knew that there were places the money should go to first. Her parents always did their best to encourage her to spend what she earned, to persuade her that they could manage on their own, that things would improve over time: when the land started yielding a bit more; when her mother's jewellery began selling into shops; when her father finally made it to the top of the waiting list for the prosthetic leg that would revolutionise his day-to-day life...

When...when...when...

She would see the gratitude and vulnerability underneath their generous, kind-hearted reassurances and would know that letting them down was never going to be an option.

But now... Now, with this arrangement in place, she would be able to achieve so much...*everything.*

Which, as she slid a sideways glance at the towering guy striding confidently next to her, Angelina between them, set the agenda for her mood. Buoyed at the thought of what this brief inconvenience was going to achieve, Kate sidelined her natural inclination to keep Dante at arm's length and allowed herself to relax.

When was the last time she'd relaxed?

As they began to explore Venice, wrapped up against the biting cold, Kate realised that she had forgotten what it felt like to let life glide past her, to live in the moment and appreciate the things around her.

Dante was a surprisingly good guide and a fount of information, which he threw at them both, nodding and pointing at various landmarks to bolster what he was saying.

'The Doge's Palace took centuries to complete.'

He pointed out all the hallmarks of the Gothic architecture, squatting down so that Angelina could follow the sweep of his hand as he contoured the perfect symmetry of the building, and feigned astonishment that she couldn't rustle up facts and figures about one of the city's most famous landmarks.

Kate's eyes swept over him as he stooped and she was a little startled when he vaulted back to his feet to capture her gaze with a frown.

'She's eight,' he murmured as they strolled towards a café for a coffee break. 'What are they teaching her at school?' But he winked when he said that and gave Angelina's hand a little squeeze.

Kate grinned and then laughed.

'They're teaching her how to be a kid.' She joined in the moment, not looking at him as she reached into the backpack she had brought to extract a sketchpad and some graphite pencils. She handed them to Angelina along with a few lighthearted instructions on drawing, as best as she could, the square in which they had been seated and which was the biggest open space in the city. From here, they were treated to the spectacular view of the stunning, elegant buildings, as old as time, that made up the city.

'Use your imagination,' Kate urged Angelina. 'The Basilica is gorgeous and so is the bell tower…but you can draw them how you see them through your eyes.'

'I will do it for you, Papa!'

'I will frame it and keep it on my desk at work.'

It was there in the sudden flash of warmth in Dante's eyes—that fierce paternal love that could be hard easily to detect.

How sad, she thought, to have all that love trapped inside, to be a prisoner of a harsh, duty-bound childhood. Had his ex-wife been the only woman who had managed to break through that diamond-hard exterior?

Curiosity clawed inside her, sudden and over-powering, and for a few seconds, as she vaguely listened to Dante explain something of the history of the piazza to his daughter, she could feel the acceleration of her heartbeat thudding inside her, confusing, disorienting and a little scary.

She blinked and what she saw was no longer the forbidding guy she had agreed to marry but the man—living, breathing and crazily, inaccessibly, stupidly sexy…

Kate screeched to a panicked halt at the image that flared in her head of his powerful, muscular body in bed with her.

Husband and wife…

Except that was going to be a two-year fantasy! And beyond that the chasm between them was so great that ever to think about breaching it would risk being swept into its cavernous depths.

The mere thought was terrifying. A lifetime spent travelling from one place to another had bred in Kate a healthy respect for staying put, for a simple, quiet life. She adored her parents, but she was very well aware of the limitations their nomadic lifestyle had conferred on them. It was one of the reasons they were where they were now, for heaven's sake!

Dante, with his suffocating, overwhelming personality and his dark, dangerous charisma was the very opposite of simple and quiet. He was a raging volcano and the line between fascination and mortal peril was wafer-thin. Gut instinct told her that, just as gut instinct had protected her for two years against the devastating sex appeal which lurked underneath the cool, remote veneer.

By the time they were on their way back to Antonio's palace, with Angelina nodding off between them, she had still not managed to quite shake the disturbing, niggling thought that a gateway had opened up, inviting her to tread inside.

'What's wrong?'

'Sorry?' Kate blinked, her almond-brown eyes locking onto his.

'You've gone quiet on me. I thought today went…well. So, tell me what's wrong.' His voice was a silky murmur that feathered through her body with the intimacy of a caress.

'Nothing's wrong,' Kate said on a sharp intake of breath, gripped by a sudden hot pulsing in her veins that left her breathless and alarmed. 'I guess I thought it might be a good idea to just sit back and allow you to spend time with Angelina.' She cleared her throat and continued in a firmer voice, even though she was still acutely aware of him in ways that panicked her. 'It's great seeing the two of you interacting.'

'Thank you for joining us.'

'You honestly didn't need me there,' she countered huskily. 'Why did you ask me along?'

'Because...' He shifted and flushed. 'A day out with Angelina... It's not something I am accustomed to enjoying. It's not familiar terrain.'

'You should do it a bit more. She loved having you with her for the whole day.' Kate half-turned to look at him and stopped breathing for a few seconds as their eyes clashed in the darkness.

'I know,' he said huskily and then smiled with tentative warmth.

'And you should do *that* a bit more,' she added on impulse. Why not? If they were going to marry for convenience, then he would be around in her life, even if it *was* for a limited period of time. And the fastest way to kill these uneasy, uninvited stirrings of *awareness* would be to get onto another track altogether.

The *friendship* track was a safe one. She would be able to engage, to smile, to socialise at his side without this unwelcome and unexpected fluttering inside her just because their roles might be a little different. She didn't know what to do with the restless stirrings inside her. She just knew that they had to *go away*.

'Do what?'

'Smile.'

Dante gazed into almond-shaped eyes the colour of milk chocolate flecked with green, and for a few seconds was utterly taken aback. Disoriented and not knowing why, he found himself staring at her, deprived of speech. What was that about... this hot stirring in his blood, the familiar way it tracked through his veins, making him restless and edgy? No, he *knew*. An inconvenient attraction, one he would have to sideline, to subdue, and subdue it he would.

In work, at play, in all the corners and angles of his high-voltage life, he was always in control. It was the way he had been raised—to keep his feelings contained, always to know where his focus lay. Inconvenient attractions? No, there was no room for them or for his eyes straying, feeding his imagination, shifting his focus. He was strong—always had been, always would be. It was the way he was, a rock hewn from his life's experiences.

Distracted, Dante succumbed to thoughts of a past he always kept locked away.

The dramatic painting might hang behind his

desk, a constant and everlasting reminder of the wife who had been perfect only on paper, and yet, despite that visual reminder, he had consigned her to a place that did not occupy a single scrap of his mind.

Luciana had been beautiful and as eligible as him. The match had been brokered by his parents and Dante had had no qualms about its suitability. Two great Italian houses would join forces. He was and never had been interested in romance. He had always known that marriage would be a simple matter of business and pragmatism, the continuity of the family line. Of course, he had had relationships with various women over the years, but he had never envisaged longevity with any of them, and in fact he had always been discerning when it came to those. Playing the field, like a kid without any parameters or sense of self-control, had never been his thing.

Had he expected his marriage to be the nightmare it had turned out to be?

Never.

He had entered into it in good faith but it had quickly become apparent that his stunning wife was utterly uninterested in him. Before the ink was dry on their marriage certificate, she'd announced she liked a varied sex life, and her assumption was that he would have no problem with that. Of course, she would provide him with an heir to the family empire, because that was part of the bargain, but that was it.

She'd done her own thing. He'd buried himself in work, gritted his teeth and wondered how long he would be able to put up with the men and women who entertained his wife. The tipping point had been reached the very second his daughter had been born, at which point he laid down some basic laws and resigned himself to a marriage in which Luciana did as she wished but with discretion, and so would he, should he so choose.

In fairness, he knew that it was a lifestyle not uncommon amongst many of his privileged acquaintances. The fact that she'd been rude to everyone she considered beneath her had been as repelling, in many ways, as her conscious philandering.

Would he have ended up pushed to the point of divorce? Or had his upbringing been so deeply ingrained that he would simply have shrugged it off and accepted the hand he'd been dealt? As many would have, and did, in the elevated circles in which they'd both moved. As far as his parents, and indeed his uncle, had been concerned, there'd been nothing amiss with the pairing.

It was a question Dante had never got to ask, because she had died in the very car crash that had taken his parents—an accident on a rainy road late at night after a trip to the opera. A distracted chauffeur. Seconds during which his future had changed for ever.

Dante frowned at the rush of memories crowding his brain and saw that the woman next to him—the woman who was to become his wife—was looking at him with something very much like empathy. As that was something he didn't need, he abruptly turned away, before moving the conversation onto more pedestrian ground.

Between them Angelina had shifted so that she was now resting against Dante's arm, gently snoring, oblivious to the hushed conversation around her.

'I meant to mention that your first social engagement is in the calendar.'

'Sorry?'

Better, Dante thought, annoyed with himself for being derailed by beguiling almond-shaped eyes and a heart-shaped face oozing just the sort of gentle understanding he was not in need of. Much safer being back in the arena of discussing practicalities.

'If you recall, part of the arrangement between us involved joint functions attended together?'

'I thought that was destined for after the big day.'

'The big day?'

'Yes. When we tie the knot and pledge undying love and devotion to one another.'

'Ah. *That* big day.' He smiled a slow, curling

smile and looked at her with dark-eyed amusement. 'Remind me...does obedience feature alongside the love and devotion?'

Kate blushed. The ice-cold guy with the killer looks clearly had a sense of humour, and that unexpectedly brought a rush of colour to her cheeks and a sharp sexual awareness that forced dampness between her thighs and made her blush even redder.

'I think all those vows might have to be tweaked,' she returned, voice hitched, still feeling the heat in her cheeks. 'What is this function, exactly? Will I be there in the capacity of Angelina's nanny?'

'You will be there in the capacity of my future wife,' Dante asserted. 'Once the announcement is made and everything is official, we can jointly break the news to Angelina.'

'Announcement...'

'Don't tell me that you didn't give that any thought?'

'Well, yes, in a manner of speaking...' Had she? Not really. She'd considered the up sides and the ramifications, but the details had all been wrapped up in that pre-nup she had signed. All other considerations had been shoved to the back of the queue for further inspection at a later date.

'I'm guessing from your blank expression that the *manner of speaking* you refer to was somewhat on the vague side?'

'Somewhat,' Kate reluctantly agreed. She thought about the sort of people she would meet, and the reality of what she was about to do hit her with the force of a sledgehammer.

She would be catapulted into a level of wealth that would surpass anything she might ever have encountered—which truthfully wasn't much, given her background. She had only vaguely seen from a distance the glamorous, expensively dressed people who circled around Dante, like twinkling stars orbiting the sun. The prospect of actually having to mingle with them made her feel a little nauseous.

'It's going to be a little odd, isn't it?' she ventured, chewing her lip and staring off into the dark distance as the chauffeur-driven car noiselessly gobbled up the miles.

'Undoubtedly it will be for you, but that's a big subject to broach in the back of a car with a sleeping child between us. We can talk about this when we are back at my uncle's,' Dante said with surprising kindness. When Kate focused she could make out the approach of the palace, its splendid pale contours as magnificent as an intricate gossamer confection.

Antonio had retired to his quarters, even though it wasn't yet seven-thirty in the evening, and as Dante lifted Angelina out of the car and carried her into the house he looked at Kate and drawled with wry sarcasm, 'My suspicion is that that sly fox has chosen to avoid a discussion on how the appointment with his consultant went.'

Kate burst out laughing.

'Would he be that devious?'

'That old man takes devious to another level.' But he was smiling with genuine affection and warmth. and

Head tilted to one side, Kate smiled back at him, because for a guy whose smiles were as rare as hen's teeth his was oddly infectious. She said thoughtfully, 'You really adore him, don't you?'

She remembered what she had been told about his parents, but that had been told to her in the strictest of confidences, even though now, with him about to take Angelina up to bed, she was so tempted to give in to curiosity.

Braced for an abrupt halt to a conversation which felt so different from most of their inter-actions in the past, she was surprised when he hes-itated. And even more surprised when he mused, 'Antonio…was the cool uncle, the uncle who blew in from adventures, filled with tales of excitement. For me? A breath of fresh air.'

'Why?'

As if she had no idea.

'Because…' He began to head up the stairs, as light on his feet as a panther, even though he was well over six feet. Kate followed alongside him, guiltily thrilled to be allowed into his thoughts and straining so that she could hang onto his every quietly murmured word. 'My own parents were very different. Austere, traditional, sights firmly fixed on the bigger picture...'

'Perhaps that allowed Antonio more wiggle room to take a different path,' Kate said, standing back as he nudged open Angelina's door with his shoulder and carried her to her bed. It was a frothy four-poster extravaganza, very much in keeping with the ornate, beautiful room, big enough so that she had her own separate play area and another room for doing her homework and relaxing.

'You're probably right. He certainly never had time for convention and so, between us, our bond was very strong. He was expected to pick up the baton within the family empire once he left university, as my father dutifully had, but as soon as that degree was in his grasp he decided that the family interests weren't sufficiently stimulating. He once confided that sitting behind a desk was no comparison to checking out what was happening in the Amazon. I think he reckoned the bookkeeping could wait—until, of course, it couldn't wait any longer.' He chuckled softly, not looking at her.

Kate watched him as he gazed down at Angelina, his expression open and revealing, the simple love of a father for his daughter, quietly murmuring confidences that were hardly confidences really, but which still felt like secrets shared. No wonder that she had been picked out for this strange assignment, she thought. Not only was it about relieving his adored uncle of his anxiety, but she fitted the bill when it came to Angelina. She was probably the *only* one who fitted the bill. He trusted her. He trusted her to look for no more than what was on the table and he trusted her when it came to his daughter.

She made the perfect fake wife.

They exited the room quietly and returned downstairs, although at the back of her mind Kate wondered whether he actually expected her to follow him. Maybe he would veer off in the direction of one of the many rooms to work, but he didn't. Instead he turned to her to tell her that there would be food in the kitchen, stuff prepared for Antonio, and that they should eat and he would explain about the function he had earlier mentioned.

'Didn't your father feel as though he'd been left in the lurch?' she asked, picking up the conversation they had started.

Dante shrugged and looked at her and she reddened as she stared back at him, their eyes tangling, neither breaking eye contact.

'I'm being nosy,' she eventually muttered. 'Of course your family history is none of my business.'

'Some might say that it very much is now that we're travelling down a different road. At any rate, it's no secret that there was some animosity between the two brothers and, yes, my guess would be as you say.

'There's chicken and pasta...but no one to do the honours.'

'You're very spoiled.' Kate smiled and took over. 'Do you know where anything is kept in this kitchen?'

'I'm familiar with the location of the wine.' He grinned back at her, and the room swam for a couple of seconds, but then she busied herself with the food that had been earlier prepared.

But she was so aware of him, alert to his presence in ways she never had been before, and keenly aware of that moment just then when they had stared at one another while an electric charge had built with agonising potency between them. Had he felt the same? she wondered.

'My theory is that Antonio, having had to take over running the family business after my parents died, is making up for everything he thinks he may have failed to do by wanting everything in place.'

'What do you mean?'

'Of course, what I say here does not leave this room...' He waited until she nodded and knew, with irrefutable certainty, that she was utterly trustworthy.

'Antonio wants me married for many reasons. The first is that he believes I need the stability of a woman because of Angelina and because, in some way, he's always been like a father to me, despite or perhaps because of his globetrotting ways. He always knew what he felt I lacked, which was the simple business of having fun, and he considered himself essential in bringing that to my life.'

Dante smiled. 'In whatever devious ways and means possible. But beyond that, this house of D'Agostino, which I'll now inherit, running along with my ex-wife's concerns, is a deeply traditional family affair. My uncle wants to ensure an easy transition now that he foolishly considers himself on the way out, and part of that, he feels, would be maintained with a wife by my side. He thinks he's sparing me the daily discomfort of all those traditionalists clucking their tongues in despair at my daughter's plight. To do him credit, they've probably been whispering for months, if not years.'

'But not to you…'

'No one would dare. I'm excellent when it comes to putting down my boundaries and no one has ever challenged them.'

'And what when the wife bails ship in two years' time?'

'Then, at that juncture, all and sundry will have realised that I am my own man and will not question decisions I choose to make. To be frank, if it weren't for my uncle's concerns and my desire to abate them, I wouldn't be considering this option right now.'

'Because you don't care what people think?'

'That and the fact that I'm not on the market for a wife—as I've mentioned. You'll be my partner, Kate, but you'll never really be my wife.'

It was a casual remark but it still made Kate shiver at the thought of a personality so untouchable, so controlled. She needed to forget about those glimpses of someone else which had given her pause for thought, had offered her an insight into the man beneath the billionaire nobleman, and remember how cold he was.

'Thank you for sharing that with me,' she said quietly. 'This food smells delicious, doesn't it?'

'It does. Antonio's chef is excellent. And as an aside…' he raised his eyebrows with amusement '… I do happen to know my way around a kitchen beyond the location of the wine cellar.'

'Oh, really?' Kate warmed to the dark eyes resting on her and flashed him a similarly amused smile, relieved that the ground was no longer shifting underneath her feet. 'I'll try to ignore all the staff you have at your house in Milan who are there to cater to your every whim.'

'Now you're just making me sound like a spoiled brat.' But he burst out laughing and, when it settled on her, his gaze held hers for a fraction longer than necessary. 'I did go to university in your country.' He sat forward to help himself to some of the food Kate had laid out for him.

'You shared a house with other guys—like a

regular person?' She tried to imagine that and failed.

'In a manner of speaking. Two friends, and the house belonged to me.'

'Of course it did.'

Dante burst out laughing again, a proper, sexy, full-throated laugh, and in that instant there was absolutely nothing cold or remote about him. In that instant, he was dangerously, thrillingly, all red-blooded male.

'So maybe you have a point.' He was still half-laughing as he spread his arms wide in a gesture of pious acceptance, 'I may be a little spoiled after all.'

'A *lot* spoiled. And I guess you also had a bunch of people waiting on you hand and foot?'

'Not in the last year of my residency,' he drawled. 'Too many bodies in the house when, at the time, I was only interested in one.'

It took her a few seconds but, when she understood what he was saying, she went beetroot-red and was lost for words, which made him chuckle.

'You have a very transparent face, Kate. I've embarrassed you.'

'Not at all. Uh…no…'

'We're both adults.' He shrugged. 'I just say it as it was. So, moving on…'

Kate was only too glad to move on. Those casually uttered words had filled her head with graphic images and made her break out in a sweat. Yes, they were both adults, but for her? No. Casual sexual experiences were not in her playbook and she had never been in any hurry to put them there.

'Yes,' she said breathlessly. 'This thing—this function—will it be big? When is it?'

'Not big, no. Just relatives, friends and then we can sit with Angelina, explain it to her and take our time doing so.' He half-smiled. 'We cannot expect a young child to keep such news to herself, and I'd rather her friends know after it's been announced to their parents, so to speak.'

Kate relaxed. She wondered whether he still harboured doubts about her commitment to this proposition, hence the necessity to formalise their agreement in the eyes of those close to him before he told his daughter. If he'd known how much the money would mean to her parents, then he'd certainly have known that backing out, for her, was not on the cards. And as for this little get together... Something small and contained would be manageable, surely? She could deal with that.

'It's been put together in some haste but—' he shrugged '—no matter. What I can tell you is that it's perhaps sooner than you might wish for, but I don't see the point in waiting, especially when I suspect my uncle isn't going to let the grass grow beneath his feet. He'll be spreading the news faster than a town crier.'

There was wry indulgence in his voice when he said that. It made her think of him as he must have been all those years ago, leading a splendid and privileged life of duty and responsibility, with Antonio the carefree genie in the lamp bringing magic and stardust to his childhood.

From her point of view, the sooner the beginning, the faster the conclusion.

'Sooner? Sooner as in…when, exactly?'

'Tomorrow evening.'

Kate's eyes widened and she looked at him in consternation.

'I'm not sure I'll be…er…mentally equipped to deal with… That's *very* soon.'

'Would waiting another week change anything?'

'Maybe not, but—'

'Excellent!'

'And so, this event is going to be here? You'd better tell Antonio first thing in the morning so that he can prepare himself.' She glanced around her, as if trying to spot a concealed army of waiting staff and platters of food, along with other warning signs of a party in the process of being arranged.

'Not here, no. The less stress my uncle has to face, the better. I have a yacht moored at the mooring pile of La Salute. Excellent views.'

'You have a *yacht* moored?'

'Small. Nothing fancy, but I suspect the guests will shun jeans and sweaters.'

'So, formal—how formal?'

'More opera than cinema. You can shop tomorrow. I'll open an account for you. You'll find that there will always be an extremely healthy balance for you to dip into.'

'Signor D'Agostino...'

'Dante. I feel that it's essential you address me by my first name, bearing in mind we're going to be married.' He shot her a slow, crooked smile that had her pulses suddenly racing. 'The fewer eyebrows raised, the better.'

'So we're supposed to be... Er, do we have to pretend...? What I'm trying to say—'

'You're blushing again. I like it. Please feel free to make a habit of it. And to answer the question you're struggling to ask—no. We don't have to hold hands or gaze into one another's eyes. Such public displays of affection won't be expected of me.'

'Oh, good.' Kate breathed a sigh of heartfelt relief, and then added with a rush of honesty, 'Because when it comes to holding hands and gazing adoringly into a guy's eyes I would want to actually be involved with him.'

'Good. I like that. No room for misunderstandings. Tomorrow, we'll leave at seven, with Antonio there a little earlier, as there are a number of relatives he hasn't seen in some time. It'll give him time to chat. And one last thing—leave the jewellery to me.'

'The jewellery?'

'You're about to enter a different world.' Dante smiled with a mixture of amusement and kindness. 'It's only fair that you have all the parts of the uniform you'll occasionally be required to wear...'

CHAPTER FIVE

NERVES KICKED IN roughly half an hour before Dante was supposed to meet Kate in the marble hall where they would be driven to the private water-taxi waiting to deliver them to his yacht.

Having relaxed the evening before at the thought of something small and contained, with just a handful of close friends and relatives to contend with, Kate had spent the day in a state of mounting nervous tension.

True to his word, Dante had opened a personal account for her, and the sum deposited had made her eyes bulge and her mouth go dry. He had texted her the name of a boutique located in one of the fashionable streets on the outskirts of the city and had informed her that she would be expected and would be looked after. She could choose whatever she wanted.

Kate took this to mean that she would be guided into the right sort of formal dress for the occasion, just in case her lack of relevant experience somehow made her go rogue and end up buying something unsuitable.

In truth, she didn't care. This was not a case of standing up for herself and demanding the right to wear whatever she saw fit. This was not any kind of relationship in any way, shape or form. This was a business arrangement—frankly, he called the shots, and why would what she wore matter to her when he was no more than a means to an end?

If she had felt the occasional, unexpected frisson in his company, then that was to be expected, because she was on a different footing with him from she had been in the past.

His choice was high-end, haute couture with no price tags on any of the garments. The implication was, presumably, that if you had to check the price, then you couldn't afford to shop there.

She was treated with bowing and scraping subservience. She was put through her paces by two terrifyingly elegant women—which she found horribly uncomfortable—before being made to try on a dizzying number of elegant dresses and make a choice.

'Perhaps,' one of the women suggested in Italian, 'You might find it helpful to take several with you, in case Signor D'Agostino has a preference?'

To which Kate burst out laughing and said, with a shake of her head, that he had already had quite sufficient input into the whole exercise, thank you very much. She didn't think they quite understood her broken Italian.

Then there was her nails, her hair, the accessories…

Several hours later, buffed and polished, Kate looked at her reflection in the full-length mirror in her bedroom suite. The girl staring back at her bore no resemblance to the one who had started the day in jeans, jumper and thick waterproof coat, eschewing the expensive purchases in favour of comfort.

That girl had been fresh-faced, make-up-free and hardly worth a second glance, as far as Kate was concerned.

This one looked five years older and was elegant, sophisticated and, frankly, unrecognisable. Her hair had been highlighted and was a rich mix of chestnut and gold, and swept up and expertly kept in place, save for some tendrils artfully framing her face. It emphasised the length of her neck. The dress, a simple cream and black silk affair, fell straight to the floor, fitted her like a glove and accentuated her slender build. It was cold, and she would wear a shawl and her cashmere coat.

Heart beating fast, Kate was captivated by the image staring back at her. She marvelled at how a simple change of outfit and a few clever tweaks to her hair could turn the nanny into…someone who was still a nanny but now appeared fit for the nobleman Dante was. Or at least, more fit now than she had been twenty-four hours ago.

She had never paid any attention to her appearance. When much of her life had been spent travelling, basking in sun one minute and huddling under the awning of a caravan in a different county the next, stuff such as gazing into mirrors and wondering what shade of lip gloss to wear to the prom were weird luxuries that had never really featured.

So now, mouth half-open, she could scarcely believe the transformation. If her parents could have seen her now, they wouldn't have believed their eyes. She suspected that they probably wouldn't have approved either. They had always subscribed to the hippy way of thinking, that *au naturel* was always best, and that the best things in life were free.

Kate breathed in sharply and her eyelids fluttered. At least, she thought, the best things in life had always been free until her father had had his accident—at which point they had all discovered that the best things in life came at a hefty price.

Hence the reason she was here, gaping at this new version of herself, with her stomach in knots.

She grabbed the clutch she had bought—one of the many expensive accessories—along with the strappy sandals which were silly, given the cold weather outside, hooked the shawl and coat over her arm and took to the stairs.

Angelina was in her room, in the safe care of one of the young members of staff who had babysat in the past, watching television. Kate had popped in earlier, making sure to keep all mention of the party to herself, as per Dante's instructions. She had hugged her tightly, tighter than usual, and had thought how odd it was that in the blink of an eye she would be a *stepmother* to this adorable little girl with her contained, sweet-natured personality. A little confused at first, Angelina had squeezed her right back and kissed her forehead in a curiously grown-up way.

Kate would be pleased to get past this tiny element of subterfuge.

She made it to the bottom of the stairs at the very moment Dante was emerging from the wing of the palace he had been using for his office.

She saw him before he saw her because he was distracted, reading something on his mobile, and because she had raced down the stairs barefoot and so had barely made a sound.

He looked...breath-taking.

His raven-black hair was swept back, accentuating the harsh, chiselled angles of his face, and he was dressed formally in a dark, bespoke suit, a white shirt open at the neck and no tie, which was the only concession to casual dress. He looked every inch exactly what he was: an aristocrat; a man who lived on a different planet from her, looked at the world through different eyes and had always, from the day he'd been born, breathed in the rarefied air afforded to the uber-elite.

No wonder this was a match that suited him, she thought, tearing her eyes away and bending to put on the sandals. She would never pose a threat, would never try and outstay her welcome, would always recognise the vast chasm between them and would never be tempted to breach it.

To all intents and purposes, she was a temporary asset that would always be invisible, and therefore in no danger of ruffling the calm surface of his day-to-day life.

Dante had not been aware of Kate soundlessly descending the sweeping staircase. He'd been too busy checking his emails, and scanning communications from the various people who had hurriedly organised the function he had set in motion. It was something that had to be done, so he might as well get it over with.

Why wait? An announcement would have to be made, and any thought of communicating the situation on the down-low was out of the question. He was a D'Agostino, after all. He could have waited a while and taken his time with the invitation list but, as far as Dante was concerned, the people he actually cared about enough to want on that prized list were few and far between. If it was all very last minute, then he was not unduly bothered about who could make it or not. In all events, not a single invitation had been turned down, such was the scope of his power and influence.

Glancing at his watch, and half-turning to the staircase, he saw Kate just as she was bending to see to her sandals…and for a few seconds the breath left him in a whoosh.

She was fiddling with the straps and his eyes followed the graceful curve of her pale neck and the slender delicacy of her arms. She was maybe five-six, and so slightly built that he felt a strong breeze could whip her off her feet. He heard her click in tongue in annoyance and snapped out of his momentary trance to walk towards her.

'Allow me.'

She smelled of fresh flowers and the scent filled his nostrils, pausing him as he knelt to attend to the sandals that had been giving her trouble.

It was an intimate gesture, touching her, kneeling at her feet, the dominant male yielding to a beautiful woman. Her ankles were narrow enough for him to circle with his fingers and her skin was soft and silky-smooth. She was wearing pale-pink polish on her toenails and it seemed ultra-feminine on her.

The straps were fiddly and he had big hands. Was that why he was having a hard time doing the things up? He was hyper-aware of her hand lightly on his back as he knelt in front of her. Eventually, job done, Dante vaulted to his feet, making sure to step back a few paces so that he didn't invade her space.

Knockout.

That was the only word for the complete picture that hit him square in the face as he looked at her full lips, small, straight nose and a heart-shaped face that lent her a look of disingenuous innocence. He felt a surge of hot blood rush through him, insistent, unwelcome and reminding him that this was not the first time his body had broken its leash and done its own thing in her presence. Everything inside him stirred in sudden hot arousal and, for a few seconds, it was such a shocking reaction that he barely recognised it. This was not part of his rigid, orderly approach to life. This was wild and uncontrolled, and he rejected it at speed, but in its wake he was left shaken and grittily confused.

'I have the jewellery,' he said abruptly, reaching into his pocket and pulling out a deep-purple velvet box.

'Okay.'

Kate had likewise stepped back, eyes wide, breathing shallow as she looked at him.

'Wow.' Her mouth fell open at the intricate, ornate diamond-encrusted necklace he held up. It cascaded between his lean, brown fingers like a tinkling, glittering waterfall of precious gems. She reached out and hesitantly touched the necklace with the tip of a finger.

'It won't bite.'

'Tell me this isn't real.'

'Not real?'

'These diamonds!'

'Why would it not be real?'

'Dante, I couldn't possibly wear this.'

'What are you talking about?'

She gazed at him and sighed at the bewildered frown on his face. Then she touched the necklace again, another quick, light touch, and he smiled, suddenly relaxed and amused at her tentative response.

'Turn around, Kate, and let me put it around your neck.'

'What if I lose it?'

'You won't lose it.'

'What if it…falls…breaks? It must be worth a fortune.'

'It's insured,' Dante said kindly. 'But it won't fall, and where will you lose it?'

'Anywhere! I might be leaning over the side of your yacht! I've never in my entire life been on a yacht before. What if I'm seasick?'

'Over the side of the yacht? I'm not seeing it, personally. If you feel nauseous, then I'll be right by your side—no problem. I'll deliver you in one piece to the rest room. Probably a better bet than running for the side of the boat. Besides—and small point of order—it's going to be stationary.'

'You're being sarcastic.'

'You're making it hard for me not to laugh.'

'I'm not used to all of this!'

'I'll be right there by you. We're in this to-gether. I'm not going to abandon you to whatever fate has in store, trust me. Now, turn around and let's get this done or we'll be late.' He leant into her and whispered with amusement, his breath warm against her neck, 'Although, I'm guessing you wouldn't say no to buying time...'

Nerves shredding at the feel of his warm breath on her, Kate hastily spun round to feel his cool fingers on her neck as he expertly clasped the priceless necklace securely. Then he walked her over to the gilt mirror on the wall and stood be-hind her, watching her as she gazed at the dia-monds encircling her neck, tentatively touching it in disbelief.

Oddly, this simple gesture made Dante's heart swell with a certain amount of pride.

'It's a family heirloom,' he said, his eyes briefly dropping to a tiny mole on the back of her neck before meeting and holding her gaze in the mir-ror. 'Belonged to the family on my mother's side. It wasn't quite ornate enough for my ex-wife's taste, so it's remained vaulted until now. It suits you—your outfit—perfectly.'

He stood back but it was suddenly an effort to look away. 'We should go.' He cleared his throat and spun round on his heels, breaking the fragile connection between them and striding towards the front door.

Caught up in a magical moment for a few seconds, Kate briskly walked towards him, allowed him to help her with the shawl and then shoved her arms into the sleeves of the coat before hurriedly tightening it around herself. She could still see the image of his dark head as he had knelt at her feet, fiddling with the thin straps of the sandals while she had done her best not to pass out.

It was cool in the night air and—in keeping with a phoney relationship, with no effort being necessary unless there were witnesses around—Dante spent much of the drive on the phone, switching languages as he discussed business, while Kate stared out of the window as the sleek car ate up the miles towards Venice.

She didn't quite know what to expect. The one thing she did know, however, was that she had to play it as cool as he did. It hadn't escaped her notice that, while she had been in a state of nervous freefall when he had stepped close to her, when his fingers had brushed the back of her neck and feathered against her foot, he had remained as cool as a cucumber.

Nor had it escaped her that he had, in passing, paid a compliment about her dress, but had he told her that she looked okay? Not a bit of it. She looked the part, and that was the key thing.

And why was that? Because he didn't *see* her—not really. Not in the way her treacherous eyes saw *him*. Not in the stupid, crazy ways that made her shiver, gave her goose bumps, made her go weak and sparked a tingle between her legs that was shameful but pleasurable.

Venice at night was stunning, a kaleidoscope of light reflecting off water, shifting and changing so that the elegant ancient buildings gazing into the canals looked other-worldly and mysterious. A city of possibilities, drenched in romance. The air was still and cold.

They were delivered to a water-taxi that was waiting for them. As she stepped out of the car, sliding past Dante's driver, who had whipped round to open the door for her, Kate felt very much like the woman that she had never imagined being. She felt like Cinderella, with the pumpkin banished to the shadows, replaced with a carriage. And gone were the chain-store clothes, swapped for the finery of a princess: the diamonds; the silk and cashmere… Borrowed clothes for a borrowed person who would, in due course, be returned to her own world, where she belonged.

But for now…? He was right. She had entered a different world—*his* world—and this was her new uniform.

Until the time came for her to give it all back.

The canals were so much calmer by night, and the bridges looking down at the waterways were so softly lit that it made Kate think of how it must have looked centuries ago, filled with dark corners and intrigue.

She could feel the warm weight of Dante's thigh against hers as they were taken to where his yacht was moored.

'There.'

Lost in thought and absorbed by the dark, shifting scenery, Kate started at his warm breath against her cheek and followed to where he was gazing.

'Your yacht.'

'Does it live up to expectation?' Dante glanced across to her, taking in her soft, delicate profile, and feeling her nerves, even though she hadn't said a word. He had worked in the car on the way but he had been aware of her next to him, gazing out of the window, and he would be lying if he didn't admit that he'd wondered what was going through her head.

He felt a twinge of guilt. Yes, this was a business arrangement, but she was young and she would be nervous. She would not have his reserves of self-discipline and cold, hard, focused inner strength. His upbringing had made him tough and the personal experiences that had followed—his ice-cold marriage to a woman for whom he had not, by the end, had a shred of affection or respect—had made him even tougher.

But beyond that, whilst this woman sent off all the right vibes of being strong and self-contained, he sensed an oddly vulnerable side to her.

Certainly, he doubted she'd ever had any first-hand, lived experience of the world she was about to enter. The women he knew would be familiar with this life. His ex, who had grown up with a similar level of privilege, would barely have glanced in the direction of the yacht. Nor would she have trembled at the touch of that diamond necklace around her neck. She would have been storing up complaints for the staff, already assuming oversights would be made. Dante had invited her parents out of politeness and had been relieved when they had made their excuses.

'Are you still nervous?' he asked, tilting her chin so that she was looking at him, trying to glean what was going through her head although, in the darkness, he couldn't make out a thing.

Kate shrugged. 'I'll get through it. As we both know, it's just part of the job.'

Dante frowned, for some reason disconcerted by that, even though he knew it was absolutely the response he should have been looking for.

'Surely there are some aspects of this that you enjoy?' His finger was still resting lightly on her chin. 'What about the shopping?'

'It's…an experience.'

'A good one?'

'A different one.'

'Can I ask you something?'

'Of course.'

'Can I ask why the money is so important to you?'

'You can ask,' Kate said evenly. 'But actually it's none of your business.'

Dante stared, rendered speechless by a response no one had ever before delivered to him in his life.

Kate belatedly shot him a placatory smile. 'You're lost for words.'

'I…' Dante raked his fingers through his hair and gazed at her. 'I admit,' he conceded with an expressive gesture of defeat, 'No one has ever spoken to me like that before.'

'*Never?*'

'Never.'

'That's probably because people are too intimidated to say what they really think when they're with you.'

'You find me intimidating?'

'*I* don't,' Kate said thoughtfully and honestly. 'But I'm guessing most people do.'

'I'll keep a close watch on how many people curtsy and bow to me when we're on the yacht,' Dante said pensively, his dark eyes glinting with amusement. 'That would be the litmus test, I guess. What do you think?'

What did she want, or more probably need, the money for?

The question lodged in his head like a burr, to be pulled out and inspected at a future time, if only to satisfy his curiosity.

'I think you're making fun of me, and I'm also beginning to think that that's something you enjoy doing,' Kate returned, but lightly. Her heart skipped a beat as their eyes tangled and held before he looked away, and she realised that they were approaching his yacht. It was huge, now that they were up close to it, warmly lit and reflecting on the sheet-calm water like an oil painting.

'The question is…' Dante was seduced into teasing her back '…do *you* enjoy it as much as I do? And, for the record, I'm not making fun of you. I respect you too much for that.'

'Then what are you doing?'

Dante remained silent for a heartbeat.

'I'm…'

What was he doing? Was he flirting with her? He wasn't a flirt. No. No way.

'I'm breaking the ice between us,' he told her with a brisk smile.

'I should have asked,' Kate said stiltedly after a few seconds, nerves kicking in big time, 'Whether your friends and relatives know what this sudden party invitation is all about.'

'Not in so many words.'

'What does that mean?'

'They'll suspect an announcement of some sort, I'm sure. Gathering all these people together at short notice…? Not something I would normally do.' He raised his eyebrows with a wry grin. 'Italian tongues have a habit of wagging.'

If he was lightening the conversation to ease her nerves, then he was succeeding. She smiled back at him and thought how good he was at this, how cool and collected at steering them into a zone where emotions were absent.

'I don't think Italians have the monopoly on wagging tongues. But what about Antonio…?'

'Has been requested to say nothing. I'd rather deliver the glad tidings myself.'

'They're going to be shocked,' Kate muttered with a grimace. 'I don't suppose anyone would have predicted that Dante D'Agostino might have picked the nanny to wed, when the line of suitable candidates probably stretched from here right back to Milan.'

'They'll accept it.' Dante's answer was unequivocal. 'And there will be congratulations all round.'

'Yes, but they're going to be horrified.' Kate chewed her lip and imagined the scenario, which was reassuring on absolutely no level. 'They'll think I'm after your money.'

'It is possible they may have a point, looking at it in the cold light of day...' Dante mused wryly.

'I'm not a gold-digger!'

'I know that.' He smiled and in passing appreciated the heated colour in her cheeks.

They had arrived but he wasn't ready for his own party just yet. The conversation was stimulating, and of course the driver of the water-taxi would be content to wait for however long it took.

'I— There's no way on earth I would ever go after anyone just because they had money!'

'Repeat—I know.'

'This is a completely different situation.'

'Kate...' his voice was gentle '... I *know*. You've been working for me for over two years. Not once have you ever been anything but professional in your dealings. I realise that you are no more a gold-digger than I am a ballet dancer.' Without thinking, he rested his finger on her chin and then absently outlined her lip before pulling back, startled at that brief, physical caress.

'We have an arrangement.' He looked away to the yacht he rarely used. 'It's one that suits us both. Don't waste time and energy worrying about what the people you are about to meet might think of you or your motives.' He smiled a warm, reassuring smile. 'You might actually find,' he murmured, 'That some of them are actually rather pleasant and accepting.'

'You would say that,' Kate muttered. 'You're not in my shoes.'

'They'd never fit. Smile at me, Kate. It'll be just fine. I won't leave you to the mercy of strangers.'

'There's no need to stick to me like glue. I mean, they're your friends and relatives. Of course you're going to want to circulate…' she protested awkwardly, but the thought of him being next to her was warmly reassuring. He was a cold, forbidding man and yet…there was a strength inside him and a natural moral compass that anchored her and brought her fizzing anxieties under control.

'Ready?'

'As ready as I'll ever be.'

'I want you to understand something, Kate.'

'What?' On the verge of rising to her feet, unthinkingly supporting herself from the gentle rocking of the water-taxi by holding onto his shoulder, she paused and looked at him.

In the darkness, his eyes glittered and his handsome face was all shadows and angles. When she inhaled, she could breathe in the woody, intensely masculine scent of whatever aftershave he was wearing.

'I would never have suggested this…arrangement…if I didn't have the utmost respect for you. Not only have you excelled with Angelina, for which I am immensely grateful, but you frankly haven't put a foot wrong. So when it comes to this…situation…you have my assurances that I consider you perfect for the role.'

He shot her a slow, crooked smile. 'I owe my uncle a debt of gratitude,' he murmured. 'And it's my dearest wish that he is healthy and happy. But I would never go so far as to wed a woman I didn't respect in order to achieve that. Self-sacrifice only goes so far.'

Respect…for an excellent employee, one who had a good relationship with his daughter…

Every complimentary word that passed his lips was a reminder that never in her life had she contemplated a marriage like this—one shorn of real emotion, one in which love was a word that would never been uttered. Her wish had always been for all the dreamy, fairy-tale stuff, for the joy of love, passion, hopes and dreams shared.

But the up sides had been too tantalising to reject. So much could be done with the money and how selfish would she have been to walk away from that?

'That's…er…very kind of you to say that,' Kate said politely.

Dante shook his head in frustration.

What was it about her? He meant every word he'd just said about respecting her. There was no way he would have contemplated this escapade—

if it could be called that—with anyone *but* her, when he thought about it.

But that polite tone of voice, with just a hint of indifference to him underlying it…

For some reason, it got under his skin.

'Shall we?'

She straightened, balancing as the boat rocked, and Dante nodded, instantly killing confusing thoughts that had no place in the scheme of things.

As the last to board, they were assured the complete attention of everyone there.

Kate knew to expect that and yet, as they stepped onto the massive yacht and walked down the stunted bank of wooden steps into the privacy of the gleaming wood, leather and polished chrome of the reception area, she felt her heart begin to gallop inside her.

She wanted to pause to appreciate her surroundings. Out of the corner of her eye, she was aware of the rich turquoise of the carpet, the polished patina of wood, the staircase to the left winding up to another deck and the twin sunken living areas with their arrangement of leather sofas.

Those things on the periphery of her vision were, however, all overwhelmed by the faces that turned to them just as soon as they were ushered inside.

The faces of a dazzling array of bejewelled, extravagantly dressed women and expensive-looking men of various ages, statures and doubtless of bank balances.

There was a hushed silence as they stood silhouetted at the entrance. Kate was vaguely aware of glass doors sliding softly shut behind them and of her cashmere coat and shawl being eased off her. In the periphery of her vision, she could see the darkness beyond the glass wrapped around the yacht, a black sky studded with distant stars like tiny diamonds and the secretive stillness of water, interrupted by reflected light from ancient buildings and bridges.

Somewhere in the crowd was Antonio and, as she searched out his familiar face, she felt Dante's arm circle her waist, drawing her closer to him.

She half-tumbled against him and felt the hardness of his body alongside hers. While she was busy trying to steel herself from going a little weak at the knees, she heard him say, in a lazy drawl and with a smile in his voice, how pleased he was that everyone could make it to his impromptu gathering.

'We all lead busy lives.' He spoke with velvety self-assurance, a man at ease addressing an audience. 'And I realise that this has been sprung on many of you. My gratitude for the effort you've all made in clearing your calendars.'

Kate recognised a platitude when she heard one. Grateful for clear calendars? This was a man for whom calendars would routinely be swept clean because no one would want to miss out on the golden ticket of a private invitation from him.

'I expect some of you may well be speculating about what I'm about to say next...' He allowed a moment's loaded silence as his dark eyes roved over a sea of curious faces. Kate, meanwhile, was toeing a thin line between rigid self-control and total nervous freefall.

'I would like to announce my engagement to this beautiful woman who has kindly agreed to be my wife.'

There was an audible gasp.

Surprise... Disbelief... Utter and absolute shock... Would anyone faint? Kate forced herself to smile, but her body was rigid with tension and she knew that she was transmitting that tension to the guy standing next to her. But how could she not be tense as a bowstring? She frantically wondered what was going through his guests' heads, all of whom would surely have known Dante's beautiful ex-wife with the impeccable pedigree.

They were standing here, confronted by Angelina's nanny—although not that many of them had even set eyes on her before. A mystery woman, she thought with shrinking self-confidence, had blown in from nowhere and nabbed the most eligible bachelor in town—or, rather, *country*.

And, just when those thoughts were swirling in her head like a swarm of angry wasps determined to cause maximum mischief, she felt Dante manoeuvre her so that she turned away from those curious eyes, turned towards him and then...

Her eyelids fluttered and suddenly she felt as though she were being dropped from a great height, so great that everything inside her was jumbled up, a swooping, diving, dancing jumble that made breathing difficult.

She was scarcely aware of raising her hands, resting her palms flat against his chest or of the way her eyes widened as he lowered his head towards her. She just felt the taste of cool lips against hers, soft and slow, and the flick of his tongue meshing with hers, wetness sliding against wetness.

It was the most erotic experience she had ever had in her life. Time stood still. Everything stood still. Everything but the rush and race of blood through her veins and the heady beating of her pulse. Hot liquid pooled between her legs until she wanted to pass out. Her body closed the small distance between them and she could feel his heat searing against her, burning a dangerous path through the cool distance she dimly knew she had to hang onto.

She breathed in deeply, and geared up to push him away gently but firmly, but he beat her to it. And in that moment she knew just how important that cherished distance between them had to be, how vital it was that she never let herself forget that this was a business arrangement and nothing more.

Still trembling, she heard him murmur with a smile in his voice, 'I knew you were nervous. I think that kiss should convince everyone that this is the real deal. Agreed?'

'Of course. Yes.'

A kiss for show…to cement this deal in the eyes of the world. No more, no less. Yet how her body had ignited. Shame flared inside her.

'Something else,' he said huskily, and then he slipped a hand into a pocket and pulled out a small, deep-purple velvet box.

Kate looked down at it numbly.

What else but a fake engagement ring for a fake engagement? she thought.

He opened the box and murmured that he hadn't been sure of the size, but there had been no time for measurements.

But, as he slipped it onto her finger, she could see that it fitted perfectly.

An oval diamond, glittering and sparkling on a slender white-gold band. There was nothing garish about it. It was the ultimate in good taste and refinement, and a thing of beauty. A searing gesture of what should have been a deeply personal and romantic moment between two people who loved one another.

'Perfect fit,' Kate murmured, raising her eyes to his, seething with resentment at the bewildering emotional response that well-timed kiss had roused in her.

She stood back and with a cool, controlled smile turned to face the mesmerised gathering, holding up her hand so that they could all admire the ring glinting on her finger.

His hand had moved to her waist—another well-timed gesture of affection. She slipped out of the casual embrace, fortified by the distance between them that kiss had put, by the ice-cold reality check it had produced.

She could see Antonio beaming and she headed towards him, pausing en route so that the diamond could be admired, and making sure she didn't look over her shoulder at the guy who had almost managed to turn her world on its axis.

CHAPTER SIX

ALMOST, BUT NOT QUITE.

Kate had had her wake-up call, and had had a few moments of utter disorientation when he had kissed her. But now…? That had been three days ago and she had had time to put that kiss into perspective.

That kiss, those casual, fleeting touches, the whole business of a ring on her finger and a life not so straightforward for the next couple of years would be a good life, as things went, she'd told herself. The joy of knowing that her parents would be taken care of the way they deserved to be in exchange for Kate leading a life of privilege that most women would give their eye teeth for. Nothing more than attendance at some functions would be required of her.

That, and of course presenting the right front to Antonio so that he had the peace of mind he needed to get stronger. She could do that. The times spent in Dante's company would be limited, although it had to be said they might very well end up doing stuff with Angelina. But would that be a hardship? No. She loved Angelina and she would set herself a mission to bring father and daughter together on slightly less forbidding and formal terms.

In fairness, as though obeying the change in their circumstances, Dante had been more present with his daughter in little but important ways. Angelina had shown her text messages on her mobile phone, which Kate had come close to suggesting might be a little too much for a child that young. She had composed responses, littered with loving emojis, and had giggled the day before when Dante had returned the favour but had got several wrong.

She had received the news of their engagement with the excitable, unquestioning acceptance of a child—no probing, no discussions. Presented with an odd and surprising development, for which there had been less than zero advance warning, Angelina had accepted Kate's new role as though it was the most natural development in the world.

'That's the best news *ever*!' She had smiled, her dark, serious eyes shimmering with earnestness. And then she had given them both huge hugs while she and Dante had looked at one another and smiled in a moment of perfectly unified compatibility.

A date hadn't been set for the wedding and Kate preferred not to think about that. It would happen and it would be the first step on a road that would reap much-needed benefits for her family.

Beyond that, she was happy to shove any unease over the arrangement to the back of her mind. What was the point in dwelling on the down sides? She had to look at the bigger picture.

The only change to her routine, at the moment, was a move from her quarters to a rather splendid suite of rooms that adjoined Dante's. The interconnecting door would remain firmly locked between them.

'Isn't that going to lead to speculation?' she had ventured the evening before, as she had turned full circle to inspect her magnificent new accommodation. When she had finally swivelled to a stop to look at him, it was to see that he was half-smiling, eyebrows raised.

'Explain.'

'We're not married yet...'

'It would no longer be appropriate for you to be in the nanny quarters now that we're engaged to be married. *That* would lead to speculation. I may have loyal staff working for me, but they might question why you're still in the servants' quarters when my ring is on your finger.'

'Servants' quarters?'

'It's a loose statement.' Dante had shrugged, unfazed by the cool criticism in her eyes.

'Is that what you've thought of me all the time I've been working for you?'

'You just said it, Kate. You were my employee. I didn't categorise you at all, if you must know. You did an invaluable job with my daughter and that was the sum total of it. Why are you offended?'

'Aren't you embarrassed to be engaged to an employee?'

'Why is this suddenly becoming an issue?'

'Stop answering a question with a question,' Kate had ground out in frustration.

'No, I'm not,' he'd said equably, which she'd found even more frustrating.

'Is that because this isn't really an engagement at all? Because it's meaningless?'

'We're past the stage of getting cold feet.' Dante's voice had been low and cool.

'I'm not getting cold feet. I just…'

'You need to stop getting lost in detail,' he'd advised smoothly but not unkindly. 'Whether you worked for me or not is irrelevant. I'm not *embarrassed* to be seen to be engaged to an employee. That's denigrating yourself. We're moving forward with this arrangement and everything is settling nicely into place. Moving quarters is just the next step. Are you…?' he had raked his fingers through his hair and looked at her with his dark head tilted to the side '…comfortable with that? I assure you, the interconnecting door will remain locked. You needn't fear that there will ever be any intrusion of your privacy.'

Kate had reddened. How much clearer could he

advertise the fact that she wasn't his type? That he wasn't attracted to her?

'We should discuss…er…'

'Timings? The business of when the knot gets tied?'

'Yes.'

'Tomorrow,' he had said. 'I have a series of meetings until five. I can be back by six and we can either have the discussion here or I can get my PA to book us a table at whatever restaurant you would like.' He had looked at her with sudden curiosity. 'What sort of food do you enjoy?'

She had met his dark, interested gaze with thoughtful eyes. It had occurred to her that this pretty much summed up the strange situation—she would be tying the knot with a guy who didn't know any of her likes or dislikes, her hopes and dreams or her moments of sadness and despair.

Then she'd thought of her chequered background. Restaurants had been few and far between. She'd smiled with genuine amusement.

'All food.'

He'd burst out laughing, which had made the breath catch in her throat, because just for a split second he had no longer been the cold, forbidding guy with the enticing proposition. He'd been a normal, sexy *human being*, a stupidly good-looking guy with a sense of humour and a laugh that made her lips twitch and had made her want to laugh out loud as well.

A guy, something inside had told her, she could like.

Confused, she had pulled back and told him that anywhere would be fine.

So here she was now, staring in the mirror before heading downstairs to meet Dante, who would be taking her to one of the most exclusive restaurants in the city.

She looked around at the exquisite suite of rooms that would now be her home for the next couple of years. The backdrop was gold and marble for rich Persian rugs and priceless antique furniture, polished so that she could see her reflection in the grain of the wood. Beyond the living area was a bedroom dominated by a four-poster bed overlooking the landscaped gardens to the back.

Kate wondered whether his wife had slept in this very room, but then dismissed that idea, because of course he would have had her close to him, next to him, sharing his space. He might have implied that separate quarters was perfectly acceptable between a married couple of a certain elevated status, but she was sure he and his beautiful wife had not succumbed to that tradition.

He had brought her closer, in keeping with her promotion from nanny to fiancée, but she would never make it past that locked interconnecting door.

For the first time, she wondered about the woman she was replacing. What must it have been like for him to have loved and lost the way he had? To still be so enamoured of a woman that he kept a portrait of her where he could always see it?

What must it have been like for his beautiful wife to have held this powerful and sexy guy in the palm of her hand?

Kate inspected her own reflection now. She'd changed. She looked the part. Her hair was nicely layered, and expertly highlighted and glossy, and her new and ever-expanding wardrobe seemed designed to do wonders for her slender figure.

The long-sleeved, deep-blue dress was of the softest cashmere and loosely belted at the waist. Her knee-high boots were bespoke. When she wiggled her hand, the diamond glittered and sparkled. She slipped on a jacket of butter-soft leather that matched the boots and headed downstairs at a brisk trot.

She hit the bottom of the stairs just as her phone beeped with a message from Dante that he would meet her at the restaurant. His meetings had overrun.

Disappointment flooded through her, which was puzzling, because it wasn't as though she had actually been looking forward to spending time with him in the back of his chauffeur-driven car! On the occasions when they had found themselves confined in the restrictive space of a car, he had barely spoken a word to her, instead choosing to work while she passed her time gazing through the window, frantically trying to marshal runaway thoughts.

There was a moment of self-consciousness as she reached the restaurant, was ushered inside and relieved of her coat. She had heard of this place. It was an intimate space cleverly partitioned by arrangements of various ferns and palms on dramatic pedestals. Nestled between these arrangements were cosy chairs and sofas, all upholstered in vivid royal-blue. The lighting was mellow and, although the place was packed to the rafters, it still managed to convey the impression of not being busy. There was a library-like hush—no loud roars of laughter or the clatter of voices competing to be heard.

She was shown to Dante's table with deference, and there he was, sprawled in one of the chairs with a glass of whisky in front of him, scrolling through his phone, which he dropped the second he realised she had arrived.

She looked spectacular—that was the punch-in-the-gut thought that hit him as soon as he spotted her dithering by the entrance. He could sense her awkwardness, just as he could understand it, although no one looking from the outside would have seen anything but cool, sophisticated elegance. She had chosen her wardrobe thoughtfully. Everything he had seen her in was streamlined and simple, and this dress was no exception. It made the most of a slender frame that was no less sexy because of her lack of curves.

There was a delicate, uber-feminine prettiness about her that only now seemed to reveal itself, although maybe, for the first time and in these extraordinary circumstances, he was seeing beyond the image she had always striven to project.

He frowned, shifted and half-stood as she approached the table.

'My apologies for the change of plan,' he murmured, watching her with brooding intensity as she settled into the chair and immediately fiddled with her hair, tucking it behind her ears and not quite meeting his gaze for a few seconds.

'That's okay.'

'Drink?'

'Water would be fine.'

'Surely not?' Dante shot her a crooked smile. 'Not when we're engaged and having a relaxed evening out...'

'Do you think people are looking at us?'

'This is a very private place, and no, despite what you may think, we haven't suddenly turned into show ponies required to go through hoops and gallop over obstacles,' Dante returned wryly. 'Forget about an audience. Why not try and relax, Kate?'

He signalled to a waiter, ordered a bottle of wine then relaxed back in the chair and looked at her for a couple of seconds. 'How are you...dealing with all of this? You've moved from the sidelines to take centre stage and I want to make sure that you're dealing with the sudden shift comfortably. Are you?'

'It's early days…'

'And the attention is only going to become more focused, I must warn you.'

'I understand that,' Kate said quietly. 'And it's worth it.' She sat back, allowing the waiter to pour them both some red wine, which he did with suitable flourish.

Dante nodded. The money… He lowered his eyes and was suddenly keen to move the situation to a different footing.

But what footing? And why?

Dante was aware of his shortcomings. He knew only too well that his austere upbringing had prepared him for a life of success, achievement and duty but had left him without any capacity for emotional generosity. His only access to what he expected was a normal childhood had been via his uncle, whom he had adored. But Antonio's occasional visits had left him gazing through a window at what love, *joie de vivre* and physical closeness might look like, unable to get past that barrier to sample those things first-hand. That just wasn't him. Perhaps, if Antonio had been more of a constant, then his influence might have been greater, but he hadn't been. He had dipped in and out.

And so Dante had long ago accepted the man that he was. It was why he had not flinched at his arranged marriage to Luciana and, whilst disappointed with the outcome, had been prepared to suffer through it, with rules laid down once Angelina had been born. He might have found her antics distasteful but, on a basic, emotional level, he had remained unscathed.

So this arrangement, this distance between them, the politeness of two strangers...why the sudden urge to change that dynamic?

'So...' He cleared his throat. 'Our wedding.'

'Yes. The wedding.'

'How does it sound that we proceed within the month?'

'Sure.'

'I've already deposited a substantial amount of money into your account. Perhaps you've checked?'

'Thank you.'

'Once we are married, I will continue to give you a generous monthly allowance, which will be independent of whatever you need for your daily requirements as my wife. But of course, that's already been confirmed in our pre-nup agreement.'

'We don't need to go over the money thing,' Kate mumbled. 'It's all perfectly fine. If you could tell me what sort of things I need to...er...do before the wedding.'

'What sort of things?'

She sighed. 'Normally a wedding is a big deal. The mother of the bride gets involved. Flowers need to be chosen, menus tasted and bridesmaids' dresses picked out.' Her breath caught in her throat and she looked away hurriedly. That was not going to be on the cards for her.

'I understand.' Dante flushed.

'What was it like first time round for you?'

'Come again?'

'Luciana... It must have been splendid.'

'It was a—a noteworthy event in the calendar for many important and influential people in Italy,' Dante said roughly. 'But that's by the by. Unless you have a particular wish to get involved in the detail, there will be a team of professionals more than capable of handling it all. Naturally, should you have any preferences with regard to flowers or decoration...'

'No.' Kate lowered her eyes.

Dante hesitated. 'Of course,' he expanded a little awkwardly, 'If your mother—your parents—would enjoy some contribution to the arrangements...?'

'What?'

'Your mother. You mentioned that there is usually involvement from the mother of the bride. I can tell you that Luciana's mother was quite detached from the arrangements for my previous wedding. It was all left satisfactorily to the army of people employed to ensure the smooth running of the event. But, naturally, in this instance—'

'No!'

Kate gulped down a fortifying mouthful of her wine and stared at him with alarm.

Dante's eyebrows shot up, to which she offered a weak smile in return.

'I'm not following you. Why the extreme reaction?' He frowned. 'Anything you feel I ought to know?'

'Anything, like what?'

'Your parents—is there a problem with them travelling here for the wedding?'

'They won't be coming, I'm afraid.'

'Why would that be?'

'Because...' She drew those two syllables out until she ran out of breath while Dante looked at her in expectant silence. 'Okay. I haven't told them.'

'You haven't *told* them?'

'I... I didn't really see the point.'

'No point...'

'It's not as though it's the real thing.' Kate rushed into hurried speech. 'And they would be disappointed.'

'Disappointed?'

'I honestly don't want to talk about this.'

'I'm sorry but I do.' He looked at her in silence and then said, in the voice of someone making up his mind, 'Indeed, I insist upon it. Arrangement this may very well be, but I don't believe in a cloak-and-dagger approach. I would also like to meet your parents.'

'No!'

'Why not? Are you ashamed of them? Of me?'

'I...' Kate tried to imagine her free-spirited parents confronted by Dante and her mind hit an immediate roadblock. They would be aghast. They would be shocked and incredulous that she had somehow fallen for the sort of guy they would privately have scorned. 'No!'

'What would happen should your parents discover at a later date that we are married? That it was kept a secret from them?'

'Why would that happen?' Kate asked uneasily. 'They don't live in this country.'

'Work with me on this one, Kate. They will find out in due course that we're married, and naturally I will be in the firing line. Perhaps they'll think that I've somehow taken advantage of you. My reputation could very well be at stake. You know from first-hand experience the importance placed on tradition and reputation in my family. I will not see that jeopardised for reasons I cannot begin to understand.'

'Yes, but...'

'I'm prepared,' Dante said quietly, 'To call the whole thing off rather than risk complications occurring later down the line. It would be inconvenient and awkward but I won't have sordid revelations rearing ugly heads at some point in the future.'

Kate gaped. She realised that in her head she had already begun to spend the money on so many things her parents needed, things that she would never have been able to help them with in a million years without it. Practical help for her father— a house which would cater to all his needs. Giving them a lifetime without guilt and fear for the future. Maybe, in time, a specially adapted caravan so that they could continue with their travels—maybe not quite as they had done in the past, but at least free from the worry that pennies spent today were pennies they might need tomorrow...

Was she prepared to derail all those dreams for the sake of a meeting? She could deal with this.

Certainly, she wouldn't be able to get them over here, but perhaps Dante and her could go and visit them for a couple of days on neutral territory—a hotel somewhere. She would have control over the situation, would make sure to steer them away from any hint that this was not a love match. They believed in love. It was what they would want for her—the very thing that they themselves shared.

She would pretend. She would waffle something and nothing about opposites attracting and then, in the blink of an eye, the charade would be over and they would understand that not all relationships lasted for ever and that opposites attracting was a recipe for disaster. That, at any rate, was a bridge to be crossed as and when in the distant future. There was plenty of time for a suitable build-up to the inevitable parting of ways, by which time their futures would be assured.

'Well, if you insist, then I suppose...although I still don't think...'

Dante wondered whether she knew that the more she protested, the more curious he was. He gazed at her in brooding silence till she ran out of steam. All the while, like a persistent undertow stirring beneath the surface, was the vague feeling that, since he had embarked on this scheme, every second spent in this woman's company revealed sides to her that were a lot more compelling than he could ever have predicted.

'Good.' He wrapped up her stammering, doubtful agreement with a brief nod. 'Overjoyed that we're finally on the same page. I'll arrange suitable cover for Angelina. I think it would benefit her to stay with my uncle outside Venice.' He half-smiled. 'They can talk weddings. Angelina can show him her bridal Barbie which she was keen to show me yesterday.'

His smile warmed, like sun melting the cool of snow. 'In due course, your parents, I'm sure, will meet her. But for now perhaps this situation would warrant just the two of us there to break the news. I suggest we leave day after tomorrow?'

'Uh...'

'Do I detect the sound of more objections being raised?' he queried with just a hint of impatience.

Kate could think of several, starting with the fact that, at such short notice, there was no way she would be able to sort out neutral territory for this meeting to take place.

'No. Not at all. I'll try and, er, find a nice hotel nearby, somewhere we can stay for—how long? A day or two?'

'I do think,' Dante offered pensively, 'That a day might be cutting things a bit short, wouldn't you agree? Even if we take my private jet, travelling that distance for a brief cup of tea seems a little excessive.'

'I'll…' Kate sighed as all exits closed. The 'brief cup of tea' would have worked, as far as she was concerned. 'I'll let them know that I'll be coming to visit, and I'll surprise them with the announcement when we get there.'

'Excellent idea.'

'Maybe,' she suggested thoughtfully, 'I could go ahead? Have a chance to, er, brief them ahead of the big reveal?'

'If that works for you.' He paused. 'Although I have to tell you that I've never found any woman so reluctant to introduce me to the people close to her. I'm presuming you have a close relationship with your family—your parents and your siblings?'

'I'm an only child,' Kate admitted.

'We have that in common.'

'That's about all.'

Dante grinned. 'Maybe we just need to dig a bit deeper...'

Kate tingled inside at the velvety smoothness of his voice. 'And, to answer part two of your question, yes, I'm very close with my parents.'

'Hence the dread of disappointing them by not presenting them with the fairy-tale dream. It'll happen for you one day. I get it. As for your closeness to them? We part ways on that front.'

Their eyes tangled and she felt heat flood through her. There was a moment of disturbing intimacy in that rare admission and it felt exciting.

'I'll confirm arrangements with you by mid-afternoon tomorrow,' he stated, flatly breaking whatever temporary spell he had put her under and she, in turn, replied with equal cool restraint,

'Okay—and, just for the record, if my uniform here is to dress up, then your uniform will be to dress *down*.'

'Is that a challenge?' Dante murmured, lazing back, looking as if he was enjoying himself.

'Maybe,' Kate murmured, lowering her gaze. 'Maybe we both have to accept challenges when it comes to this...arrangement.'

Which didn't help when, three days later, Kate found herself at the small station that serviced the nearest town to where her parents lived.

It was bitterly cold. Light snow was falling, an ominous scattering of flurries, like an appetiser for what was to come.

She wondered what might be going through Dante's head. His original plan had been to follow her out and allow her some breathing space to set the scene with her parents. Vital breathing space, as far as she was concerned, because she would be able to use that brief window to assuage potential apprehension about the speed of her mysterious engagement...whilst simultaneously planting a few useful seeds about having her head in the clouds and barely being able to think straight. She hoped that would generate dark forebodings about marrying in haste and repenting at leisure.

As it happened, everything had changed at the last minute. A series of urgent meetings with the board members of the family empire had been expedited by two weeks because of unrest in the ranks following Antonio's announcement that he would be stepping down. As the successor to the proverbial throne, Dante had informed those fractious elements within the various companies that he would be giving them a fortnight to get their heads together and table whatever questions they might have about the way forward.

'So I'll come out with you,' he had informed her hours before she'd been due to leave, thereby putting paid to any hopes for a relaxing trip back. 'It will give me an extra two days out there and I can return earlier, get prepared for a lively board meeting. You, of course, may stay on as you wish.'

'I…maybe…' Kate had prevaricated, as she had wondered what else could go awry.

The weather, she thought now, gazing worriedly at the heavens. The weather could go awry. It often did in this part of the world, where fields, mountains and rivers met the open blank canvas of a horizon only intermittently interrupted with towns and small villages.

She had hummed and hawed and in the end told him very little about her parents. When she thought about him meeting them and the inevitable awkwardness, she felt sick. Part of her expected her parents to be quiet and overwhelmed, saving their disapproval for when she was on her own, and that would be fine. A couple of days of stilted politeness would be bearable.

'It might have been a better idea to be driven here, wouldn't you agree?' Dante murmured from next to her and she snapped her attention to him. He was dressed for the cold but in the manner of someone not accustomed to having to put up with it too much—overcoat, dark jeans, a dark polo and some shoes that were not recommended for tramping through slush.

The station was busy and she could see people glancing at him with curiosity. He stuck out like a sore thumb. She had dumped the fancy gear in exchange for the clothes she normally wore in this part of the world and was sensibly dressed in various layers with a waterproof and heavy-duty, *faux*-fur-lined boots. It was late January, and she had known that winter here would not be nearly as polite and cheerful as winter in Italy.

Even in the first-class compartment, the train had not been a luxurious experience, especially when she compared it to their last luxurious joint experience, which had been on his yacht.

'Certainly not,' she said stoutly and, when his eyebrows shot up, she added for good measure, 'This is what travel is like here.'

'Really?' Dante murmured drily. 'And so nothing to do with the "dressing down" instructions you issued before we left…'

'Which,' Kate countered sarcastically, 'I note you didn't take on board.'

'If you look, you'll see that I'm wearing boots and jeans.'

'They're designer,' she scoffed and Dante grinned.

'Was that not allowed? I can't quite remember.'

'We should go get a taxi.'

'Will there be a rank of them?'

'Possibly not *a rank*,' Kate admitted, leading the way and huddling into her waterproof as the snow began to gather pace.

'Kate,' Dante said gently, slowing her down so that she reluctantly turned to him. 'Why not let me to handle this?'

'What?'

'Let me get someone to collect us from…remind me what this station is called?'

She told him and then said sceptically, 'How are you going to materialise a driver from thin air?'

'You'd be surprised what I can achieve.'

He pulled out his phone, spoke for a few minutes in rapid Italian and then looked at her smugly.

'That's very unattractive.' She tilted her chin and out-stared him, and his grin broadened into a laugh, which continued as they walked through the small, bustling station out into the forecourt.

'What is?'

'No one likes a know-it-all.'

'That being the case…shall I take the chauffeur-driven limo and let you arrange your own transport to your parents' house?'

But he was looking around as he said that and there was amusement in his voice.

Naturally, there were no taxis outside, and their wait for the car he had ordered was short, a matter of twenty minutes before a sleek, black car pulled up.

'How on earth did you manage that?' she asked, impressed.

'Easier than you probably think,' Dante admitted, ushering her into the back of the car. 'I have extensive contacts with various driver services across many continents. I telephoned my PA and asked her to arrange for us to be collected here.

The car would simply have to come from the nearest city. It was far speedier than I anticipated, so it's likely they had finished a trip somewhere relatively close. Why are you so jumpy about this?'

The car was warm and comfortable and Kate turned to find him gazing at her with an inscrutable expression.

She opened her mouth and then hissed a sigh. 'We have this…arrangement,' she said with a helpless gesture. 'I just didn't want to… I wanted to keep it over there…'

'So you said,' Dante drawled, settling back against the cream leather and gazing at her thoughtfully. 'What other little surprises are lying in store for me, I wonder?'

Here they were and, like an onion, the layers peeled off revealed yet more layers underneath.

Was this what he had anticipated?

No. In his world, women had always been remarkably straightforward, including his ex-wife, despite her outrageous and distasteful behaviour.

He had vaguely seen this as travelling down the same road with a woman who would be as predictable in her likes and dislikes as the many who had preceded her.

He had offered an arrangement that included more money than anyone could wish for and had closed the door on any unforeseen complications. It would be a simple trade-off—a huge sum of money, which she clearly wanted or needed, in exchange for a marriage in which no demands would be made on her. There'd be nothing beyond some public engagements and behind-the-scenes, mutual politeness and respect. His uncle would be happy, the traditionalists who sat on the family board would be happy. Angelina would be happy. Everyone would be happy and for him— there would be relatively little change in his life.

'I never expected you to actually meet my parents.'

'That would seem naïve to me, considering we're about to embark on two years of wedded bliss.'

'Two years being the operative words…'

'Generally speaking,' Dante murmured, 'I would never have expected my role as husband-in-waiting to be heralded with so much trepidation and alarm. I'm thinking that many parents would not have slammed the door in my face.'

'That's because you live in a world where you're surrounded by people who would do anything to be in your company.' But he was right—he was the ultimate catch. 'My mum and dad…'

'I'm listening.'

'Well, you'll have to wait and see, but please don't be offended if the welcome isn't as effusive as you probably think it's going to be.'

'Thank you for the words of warning.' Dante smiled and rested his eyes on her, taking her in, from the delicate pink of her cheeks to the sweet fullness of her parted mouth, and liking what he saw.

'Just keep quiet,' she said. 'And leave the talking to me.'

His smile broadened and she blushed beetroot-red as he looked at her with lazy, leisurely interest.

'Why not?' Dante agreed, amused. 'I can't remember the last time I was given orders by a woman. But I am certainly willing to let you take the lead, Kate, and discover where it will go...'

CHAPTER SEVEN

THE SNOW HAD been a graceful reminder to Kate of what winters could look like in Lancashire, in the tiny, off-the-beaten-track town on the outskirts of which her parents lived. It had gathered pace by the time the houses, shops and lights of the small town centre had been left behind.

It was slow going—always was. From the chaos and adventure of a life spent travelling, her parents had ended up living in the most secluded and remote spot they could possibly have found, their only link to the place a tenuous connection via Kate's mother's side of the family. Her aunt and cousin still lived there and, in fact, had been very kind over the long weeks and months. That said, they lived in one of the busier parts of the county, and it was a trek visiting her parents.

Sitting next to Dante in the back of the cab, Kate wondered what was going through his head. She didn't want to look at him. He came from the very upper echelons of Italian society and was accustomed to a life of sophistication and luxury—

a life filled with people waiting on him hand and foot, moving from one exciting city to another, always surrounded by bright lights and the very best that money and influence could buy. What on earth must he make of this slow and tortuous trip from a tiny provincial station where, at this time of the year, he could be forgiven for thinking that the majority of the population had upped sticks and left because everywhere was shrouded in darkness?

His prolonged silence was saying it all, as far as Kate was concerned. 'It doesn't usually take so long,' she eventually blurted out, turning to look at him, and then past him into swirls of snow rushing against the windows.

'Is this where you grew up?'

'I... Not exactly.'

'It's difficult to see what the place is like,' Dante confessed. 'It's very—quiet. Is it always this quiet? Is it somewhere that comes alive in summer?'

He sounded dubious.

'I know it probably seems dull in comparison to what you're used to,' Kate said defensively, 'But it's beautiful here. As beautiful as Venice, in fact. A different kind of beauty, but equally stunning. The greens of the trees in summer and the colours of the hills in autumn are spectacular. Out here, in this part of the world, it's all open spaces and you can breathe—really breathe.'

'Kate,' Dante said softly, 'What I say is not meant as a criticism. And, for the record, why do you imagine that I would find it dull out here?'

'Because...' She was ensnared by the glitter of his dark, dark eyes resting thoughtfully on her face. For a while she forgot all about the snow outside and the silent, slow progress of the car through the unlit side roads bordered with fields and open space.

'Because?'

'Because you grew up with everything.' Kate breathed, held captive by his gaze and with her heart picking up pace until she began to feel faint. 'You've lived a life wrapped up in luxury. I should warn you that you might not find the living standard out here quite the same.'

'You are telling me that I am a snob?'

'Of course you are, Dante. Why wouldn't you be?' She was genuinely perplexed that he might see himself as an ordinary human being. When she looked at him, he was so obviously offended that she blushed madly and smiled.

'If you knew half the people I knew growing up, then you would probably redefine your description of a snob,' Dante said wryly.

'What do you mean?'

'To be a snob is to consider yourself superior to other people, to put yourself on a pedestal above other people. You're very much mistaken if you think that this is the man that I am.'

Dante paused, considering yet another plunge into confidences he was not accustomed to sharing. 'I—I was raised to be the very person you describe,' he continued slowly. 'And maybe Antonio was my saviour. He escaped the constraints of birth by denouncing everything and he brought that taste of freedom into my life when I was growing up. Yes, I grew up surrounded by everything money could buy, but would I describe my life as a happy one? Possibly not.'

'What do you mean?'

'It was a cold upbringing, you might say …' He looked at her in brooding silence for a few seconds and was suddenly disoriented—by the snow and the darkness, or by her? By those calm, intelligent eyes resting on him, not pressing him for confidences and yet luring him into giving them. 'And then there was my marriage.'

A first for everything, Dante thought. A first for him. He had never spoken to anyone about Luciana. He had never been tempted to. But now, here, it felt pretty good just to utter those words, a prelude to a confidence he might regret. Who knew?

He was staring down from a great height, not sure why he was so willing to break with the script, and that uncertainty was also a first for him.

'I'm so very sorry,' Kate murmured quietly, reaching out on impulse to cover his hand with hers and barely conscious of the gesture. 'Sorry for you and sorry for Angelina. She was a very beautiful woman and you must have loved her very much. You have that wonderful painting hanging where you can see her, be reminded of her, all the time. If you'd rather not talk about it, then I'll fully understand. I know we're here and doing this—*thing*—but that doesn't mean we have to breach whatever boundaries we have.'

'This *thing*...' He raised his eyebrows. 'You have a very special talent when it comes to denting my ego.'

'Maybe that's healthy for you,' Kate returned without pause for thought and then she laughed at herself. 'Now I sound like the teacher I am.' She expected the conversation to swerve away from the intensely personal road it had travelled down, and was already waving goodbye to a million and one unanswered questions buzzing in her head, but he looked at her seriously after a short while and raked his fingers through his dark hair.

'It was an arranged marriage,' Dante said thoughtfully. 'Two dynasties uniting—expected and welcomed.'

'You agreed to that?'

'It may seem alien to you but—' Dante shrugged '—in my world, it's the done thing. It was an arrangement that worked well enough with my own parents. Unfortunately...' his lips thinned

'... Luciana was not the sort of woman willing to do anything whatsoever for the greater good.'

'What do you mean?'

'I mean my ex-wife was a sensationally beautiful woman who knew not just the power of her own looks but the immense control that came when money was aligned to that beauty. She inhabited a world in which the only person worthy of consideration was herself.'

Kate remained silent. Many things suddenly fell into place, starting with Angelina's lack of interest in talking about the mother she had lost, and ending with her absolute devotion to her father, even though he could be so remote and so engrossed with his work. Angelina had never bonded with a woman who had probably never bonded with her. On the rare occasion when Kate had asked her about her mother in passing, she had not been so much angry, upset or tearful as indifferent.

'But you have a portrait of her...'

'It always makes sense to be reminded of mistakes made. How else do we learn?'

'But that's so...so extreme.'

'For you, perhaps. For me, it's practical. We learn and we move on.'

And *that* was why he was an island, why he would never allow himself to give his heart or his emotions to any woman: why this situation made complete sense to him. Not only had he been raised to put duty first but his one and only foray into marriage had been a disaster. So now, with her, he had nothing to lose. They were on the same page, she thought, except...

She frowned and thought of her own misgivings and was uneasily aware that things might not be quite so straightforward for her.

'You must have had your own learning curves in your life?' Dante murmured.

'None as dramatic as yours. Thank you for telling me about her. We're in this together and it helps knowing a bit about each other.' She thought of her parents and was less hesitant about him meeting them now. A little bit shared had put things into perspective. His perfect life hadn't been quite as perfect as she'd expected and hers... Well, he would discover soon enough that hers contained its own twists, turns and unexpected corners.

She could see a way to them having something of a friendship. Maybe it wouldn't be marriage the way *she* understood marriage, but they would mug along until the time came for them to go their separate ways.

She took a sidelong look at his dark, handsome face and wondered about those women he would take—discreet dalliances to sate a physical appetite...

She shivered, tingled and suppressed a surge of inappropriate curiosity.

That kiss—she could still taste it on her mouth

and when she thought about that she felt faint. A proper relationship with this man, she thought—the touch of his mouth on her for real and the heat of genuine passion leaving him weak with want—what would that be like?

It was such a silly, a fleeting moment of disorientation, that she almost laughed out loud.

'Indeed,' Dante murmured.

Still half-wrapped up in inappropriate thoughts, she projected to the sleeping arrangements awaiting them and knew that at least there was no need to worry on that front. The bedroom was so small she couldn't have swung a cat in it and the bed was a single, just big enough for her to sleep in if she didn't move around too much. He would be on the pull-out sofa in the living room, and when she thought about what awaited him she wondered whether she should warn him in advance. What if he clocked where he was going to sleep and collapsed on the spot? She couldn't resist a smirk; paramedics weren't exactly a dime a dozen out in this neck of the woods.

'We're nearly here.'

'How can you tell? Everywhere looks the same.'

'Maybe in the snow,' she admitted, 'But I've been here a thousand times. I recognise the landmarks even when the weather's like this.'

'There are a lot of questions I should have asked,' he said ruefully.

'Too late. Like I said, if you let me carry the conversation, then it'll be fine. It's not as though you're going to be sticking around for long anyway.'

'Just time enough for me to break the news before I disappear on urgent business.'

'You're a very important person,' Kate said, and her heart sped up a little as their eyes tangled in shared amusement.

'So I am,' Dante agreed.

'You should tell the driver to take it easy up the lane,' she warned as the trees closed in around them, shadowy silhouettes buffeted by the snow, which was now falling thick and fast. When she looked at him, he was staring out of the window, oblivious to her.

Her parents' tiny house loomed into view, ablaze with lights, which was a useful guide to the driver, because everywhere else surrounding it was plunged in snow and blizzard-dark. The car pulled to a slow stop and, as it did, Kate saw the front door open and there was her mum, huddling in a cardigan, her long hair swept to one side. For a few seconds, she was overwhelmed with love and affection.

'We're here.' She turned to Dante but then scrambled out of the car without giving him an opportunity to respond.

Dante hesitated.

He didn't know what he had expected, and he wished he'd asked a few more questions, although events had happened more speedily than he had anticipated. He had also been lazy. Lazy in assuming that it would be straightforward to present this as a business deal of sorts, that he would be dealing with a woman with no hidden corners and no particular story to tell.

He'd been lazy and locked up in an ivory tower which he had built around himself over the years, from childhood. He seldom thought of his childhood, because acceptance of his destiny had been bred into him but just for a second he recalled the lack of physical affection from his parents as something solid, sad and tangible. He remembered childhood anxiety at always having to show a certain face, to maintain a certain stance from the day he could walk and talk. He had grown up tough, hard and self-contained. But as he looked at his wife-to-be rush out of the car, hurtling like a kid towards the slender woman framed in the doorway, and watched the loving embrace between them, something inside him hurt.

He quickly stifled that and swept out of the car, knowing that the driver would follow with the bags, including the very expensive, hand-blown glass vase he had brought with him as a gift.

He was swept inside in a tide of warmth and welcome, swept into a house that was smaller than his bedroom, in which a tiny entrance hall gave way to a small sitting room on the right. Beyond that, he guessed, was a couple of bedrooms and a kitchen.

From behind the vibrant, youthful woman with the smiling face shuffled an equally smiling middle-aged guy with a greying ponytail. Then more hugs, embraces and questions came at them from every angle.

'Amanda and George... Come in! So cold outside... So, so pleased to meet you... The minute Katie said she was bringing someone to meet us, we knew...'

Her father had lost a leg but was speedy with a crutch. Dante wondered when that had happened. Neither could get enough of their beloved daughter. Honestly, he had never experienced anything like this in his life before; he had never felt such effusive love and affection, in which he was unquestioningly and generously included.

This was family life at its very best, he realised with a sense of wonder and a wrenching feeling of loss.

It was everything he had never had.

It was as well that he had been instructed to leave the talking to Kate, because for once he found that he was lost for appropriate words.

He gleaned some things in passing. He watched the interaction between parents and daughter with intense, brooding interest, and responded with charm to the questions asked, while wondering what spin Kate would put on this manufactured relationship.

And a conscience that had not bothered him at all before kicked into gear and gathered pace, even as the evening drew to a close after a magnificent meal and Prosecco to celebrate the news they had clearly been expecting.

'So, we have a little surprise of our own for you two love birds!' Amanda carolled, bringing them into a warm huddle while George watched from the sidelines with a broad grin.

Tuned in to every nuance of the woman by his side, his wife-to-be, Dante could sense her apprehension and he shifted closer to her and swung his arm over her shoulders, instinctively protective.

'A surprise?' Kate ventured fearfully and her mother burst out laughing.

'Couldn't talk the woman out of it!' Her father growled. 'But it made sense.'

'What? What made sense?'

Dante's arm around her was reassuring. The evening had been as she had expected. Her parents had correctly second-guessed the surprise she'd had in store for them when she'd told them she was bringing a guy for them to meet, and that they might need to sit down for the news. She'd never brought any guy back for them to meet, so joining the dots hadn't been too difficult.

The only surprise was the lack of judgement.

They must have guessed how rich Dante was. That mega-expensive vase had said it all, not to mention the designer stuff unceremoniously dumped on the coat hooks by the front door as soon as they'd blown in from the snow outside. Yet neither of her parents had said anything remotely snide or derogatory about *'people who have more money than sense'*.

Kate wondered uneasily whether they were keener than she'd expected at her bringing some guy home. She was still young, but had she missed little signs that they were anxious about the effect of their peripatetic lifestyle on her? Were they just so relieved that she was *'doing what girls her age should be doing'* that they were happy to overlook Dante's exclusive background?

And, wow, had Dante played the part! Not that he had had to do much at all—just be there, so damned solid, oozing sincerity and charming the socks off both of them.

That he was rich was something they must have gleaned but she doubted either of them had any idea just how rich. Their darling daughter had fallen in love with a guy they liked, and with that all other concerns had been dusted off and stored for some later date.

'You'll find out soon enough.' Her dad winked and she quailed.

'We might not have much, Katie, darling,' her mother said, watery-eyed. 'But the minute you told us that you were bringing a chap home for us to meet, we knew it was the real deal, and your surprise… Well, grab your bags, kids, and head out to the cabbage patch! But you'd better run. This snow's getting heavier by the moment!'

'I'm sorry.'

Kate was appalled. Not ashamed, but appalled, because *now* what happened next? And what on earth had possessed her parents to present them with *this*?

Of course, she knew. They had presented her with her own private space—at great cost, because they just couldn't afford to rent one of these things.

Kate looked around at just the sort of thing she remembered from her childhood—a tight space with a fold-down double bed, a little kitchenette, a compact bathroom and somewhere to sit and relax, a pair of grey sofas that faced one another. In actual fact, it was huge compared to some she could remember.

'Why?'

'I wasn't expecting this.' Her eyes welled up at her parents' kindness allied to the nightmare of trying to work out how the sleeping arrangements would work. The howling blizzard was almost strong enough to buffet the caravan.

'You were nervous.' Dante looked around him,

spied the fridge and opened it to find it fully stocked. 'I could sense it.'

'Can you blame me?'

'No. Let me pour you a glass of wine.'

'How could you sense it?' She took the glass he poured out and offered. She needed it. Nerves had stopped her from drinking all but a single glass of Prosecco earlier, but now she needed this.

She sat and waited as he perched opposite her, so close that their knees were practically touching.

'It puzzles me,' Dante admitted truthfully. 'There seemed to be some sixth sense at work.'

'Well, you were right,' Kate said glumly. 'They're so excited for me. For *us*.'

For a few seconds, their eyes tangled before he lowered his lush lashes, concealing his expression.

She realised that she'd been so anxious that she had almost forgotten how beautiful he was, how darkly, dangerously handsome. But she remembered at pace as she breathed him in and noted the confined bedroom space just behind.

Even casually dressed and dishevelled after travelling he remained drop-dead gorgeous, his raven-black hair spiky and a little damp, his harsh, arrogant features softened as he looked at her curiously. If she was going to put money on establishing a firm friendship with this guy, then she was going to be down by her life savings if she carried on staring at him like this. But her eyes were glued to his face and it was an effort to tear them away.

'I see that. It was…unexpected.'

'I bet you think that everything about today has been unexpected. Starting with the weather and ending with us spending two nights in a caravan. Unless… Would you consider rushing back to Italy tonight for an emergency?'

'An emergency what?'

'Meeting? They understand that you work hard.'

'Not hard enough to risk life and limb, and at any rate the driver has decamped to the nearest hotel for the next couple of days. It would be unfair to have him risk *his* life and limb to fetch me for a non-existent meeting. The money…is it to help your family?'

Kate cradled the wine glass and stared down into the deep claret liquid. 'There was an accident,' she said softly, 'Some years ago. My dad was thrown from his motorbike and he lost his leg. I should explain that my life has been…unconventional. A lot of travelling.'

She breathed in deep and retraced her past, realising that it was the first time she had ever really spoken about it to anyone. She told him there had been no steady friendships along the way, that she had not remained in one place next to anyone long enough for her to consider them an anchor or a soul mate.

It was strange that she would choose this man to open up to but it felt good—dangerously good. And he made a terrific listener, not interrupting, just hearing her out with his head tilted to one side and his eyes thoughtful, sipping red wine and settling into his surroundings without a hint of condescension or snobbery. The snow swirled outside but in there the portable heaters were winning a battle to keep the small space warm.

'And yet you found time to study? To get qualifications?'

'I enjoyed it.'

Dante looked at her for a while in silence, then he drained the wine, glanced around him and wondered aloud whether she might give him a tour of their new surroundings.

'Not only can I do that, but I can do that without moving from where I am.' She eyed the sleeping area which was partitioned off with a gaily printed curtain. 'You'll have to take the sofa, I'm afraid. It should have been the sofa in the house, which might have been a bit more comfortable...'

'Was that the plan for the happily engaged couple?'

'I only have a single bed in my room. It could never have fitted both of us.' She blushed.

'What are your plans for the money?'

'I...' Kate lowered her eyes 'I... There's a mortgage on this house which I've been servicing. My parents, like I've just said, never really planned for their future. I want to make sure they're okay. More than that—I want to make sure they have the best kind of life they can have, after what's happened, and that means no money worries. There are so many things I want to get for them, too many to quantify on the spur of the moment.'

'Can I tell you something?'

'What?' Kate asked cautiously.

'Had you simply asked me for the money to do as you have just explained, I would happily have lent it to you or given it to you. Immaterial.'

'I would never have done that! Are you crazy?'

'It's an offer not many would have refused.'

'As I've already told you,' Kate said with a shaky laugh, 'You mix with all the wrong people.'

Dante smiled back at her and her heart skipped a couple of beats. 'In which case, I'm a lucky man to have found you,' he murmured, then he added quickly, 'I'd like to say that, if you want to renege on this arrangement, then I'll honour the pre-nup agreement we made without hesitation.'

Kate burst out laughing. 'Again, you're being crazy.' She sobered up and looked at him thoughtfully. 'I could never accept anything from you without knowing that my half of the bargain had been met.'

'Up to you,' Dante murmured half to himself but his dark eyes were shrewd and watchful. He slapped his hands on his thighs and stood up, which instantly made the caravan shrink to the size of a matchbox. 'So I get the sofa,' he said, eyeing it with scepticism.

'I'm afraid so.'

The logistics threatened to overwhelm her but then she decided that there were sufficient partitions to make the awkwardness bearable, and if need be she could always decamp to her own bed on some flimsy excuse or other. Developing a nasty cold and not wanting to spread it might be weak as excuses went but it could very well do.

She hesitated but was grateful when he seemed to take everything in his stride, moving to take the glasses to the sink. He told her that she should head into the house for a shower and by the time she returned he would be on the sofa, and they could both get as good a night's sleep as possible given the circumstances.

'You can say that I have a couple of urgent calls to make,' he instructed. 'As a workaholic, I am sure they won't be too surprised that I've dispatched you for a short while so that I can complete them.'

And he was true to his word.

When Kate returned forty minutes later, in her flannel pyjamas with a thick waterproof to hold off the snow, it was to find that he had hunkered down on the sofa. There was one lamp on and his shape was a dark bulk, half-hanging off. He was far too big for it, and guilt slammed into her, because the bed was a double, nicely done up for them both. Her mum had scattered petals on the duvet in anticipation of the glad tidings.

This was a decent and generous guy with a good heart, whatever her misconceptions about him had once been. Yes, he could be cold and remote, but he could also be considerate and kind.

She might get goose bumps because he was just so stupidly good-looking—and she was, after all, only human—but he didn't fancy her, so why should she refuse to share a bed with him? Why should she force him to try and sleep on a sofa that was too short and too narrow to accommodate anyone of average build?

Why should she act weird?

She quietly slipped off the waterproof, breathed in deep and nudged him on an arm.

'Problem?'

'It's stupid for you to sleep on this sofa.'

She watched as he propped himself up on his elbows. He was wearing a black tee-shirt which, as items of harmless clothing went, somehow managed to emphasise his muscled arms and the sinewy strength of his forearms, turning it from a harmless item of clothing to a flimsy garment highly dangerous to her peace of mind.

Her mouth dried and she hesitated. 'Don't worry about it. I'm fine.'

'No, you're not.' His polite reassurance made her stubbornly more determined to do what was right. 'You'll wake up with cramp in every part of your body if you sleep on the sofa. You can use the bed. It's big enough for both of us. We're adults, and we both know what the deal is even if no one else does. Besides, we'll be playing this game for a while to come. What if we get invited somewhere overnight as a couple and we're stuck in the same bedroom? What then?'

'You make a valid point.'

She spun round, padded towards the bed and slipped under the duvet, pleased that her pyjamas couldn't have covered more of her body, and if she happened to be braless under the top then it was hardly as though she was endowed with breasts the size of cantaloupes. Often enough she skipped wearing a bra.

She sneaked a glance at him as he followed in her wake in the black tee-shirt, black boxers... and a body that was designed for salacious flights of fancy.

But this was the pact they had made, and this situation was one that had to be navigated, because she was certain that it would occur again at some point in time. Best get it over and done with.

But she still felt the weight of him on the mattress and the way she had to tighten up to stop herself from sliding towards him, and she was horribly aware of the snow falling outside like a silent, white, all-concealing veil.

And, in her head, she still had the image of him

in that black tee-shirt and those black boxers, lean, brown and powerfully built.

His soft breathing was as intrusive as a fog-horn and she was conscious of every slight shift of weight until, at last, she managed to fall asleep.

CHAPTER EIGHT

KATE WOKE TO something unfamiliar, and it took her a few seconds for her brain to engage sufficiently to work out what that something unfamiliar was—arms around her, heavy and hot, and her head resting against a hard, male torso.

She froze and with each passing second it became evident that at some point during the night they had slid together. Maybe the cold had kicked in and they had gravitated towards one another in an unconscious attempt to stay warm. Or maybe his weight had ended up drawing her towards him despite her best efforts to cling to the side of the bed.

Did it matter?

She was here, with him pressed against her, and she was beginning to break out in a light, fine perspiration. She began gently easing herself away. The thickness of her prim and proper flannelette pyjamas, which would have made any Victorian maiden aunt proud, was scant protection against an imagination that was running wild. It was stampeding through all that nonsense she had preached to herself about it being no big deal to share a bed with the guy when she would probably end up having to do it at some point in the future.

She had somehow concluded that his ridiculous sex appeal was something she could acknowledge but essentially remain unaffected by because, in her head, the real power of attraction could only work if it was harnessed to genuine emotion. And, in the case of Dante, she had no feelings towards him. She was involved with him because of a suitable arrangement but that was about the extent of it.

She'd been wrong.

Every nerve in her body was ablaze with something powerful and frightening as she continued to quietly wriggle away from his heavy embrace.

She had no idea what the time was but the snow was still falling and it was inky-black through the windows.

She felt his arm tighten around her and, when she inched her head to take a look, she started because he was looking right back at her.

'Where are you going?'

Dante, who slept as lightly as a cat, had awakened before Kate had even begun her tentative withdrawal. But, instead of pulling back from the highly unnatural position in which he'd found himself, he had stayed put, enjoying the feel of her against him, as slight as a reed and as delicate as an orchid.

She smelled fragrant. Half-asleep, half-awake, he had breathed her in, enjoying the flowery, clean scent and absently linking it to her absolute lack of artifice.

Dante did not share his bed with anyone. Even when he'd been married, Luciana had had her own quarters. Twenty-four-seven intimacy had never been on his agenda. Towards the end of their short, disastrous marriage, intimacy had become an abstract concept bearing no relation to real life, because the very sight and sound of his ex had made him grind his teeth in frustration and despair.

'Dante, this isn't working.'

She flipped over and he drew back, although it was a small bed and he was still so close that she could feel the warmth of his body. He also still had his arm lightly draped over her, resting in the dip of her waist. She tapped it with her finger and then nudged it away.

'It's a small bed. Some physical contact is probably going to happen. Are you bothered by it?'

'No! But...'

'Then why do you say it isn't working?' He paused and, in a voice thick with pseudo concern, asked, 'Have I unconsciously done anything during the night to provoke your concern? I haven't made a pass at you, have I?'

'No!'

'Good! I thought that perhaps, in the dead of night and half-asleep, I might have...'

'Nothing of the sort!' Kate was wildly flustered and fast regretting that she had opened the conversation at all when she could simply have shifted away from him and fallen back asleep.

'That's a relief although, as I've already assured you, I'm an intensely disciplined man. Plus, as you've quite rightly pointed out, we're destined to share a bed at some point in time. It's inevitable, and foolishly something I hadn't factored in.'

'Yes...'

'There will be work-related events...family situations... Something as straightforward as staying with my uncle might very well require us to share a bedroom, and not all those bedrooms will have sofas large enough for me to occupy. I don't think it's going to be feasible to issue a short questionnaire on the contents of other people's guest quarters every time we accept an invitation that requires an overnight stay.'

'Granted, but...'

'The key question I feel I must be asking is whether I make you nervous. Do I? I wouldn't want you to feel unsafe with me lying here next to you.'

His voice was low and soft with the dark, velvety smoothness of the finest chocolate and it brought her out in a delicious cold sweat.

'Unsafe?' Kate was swamped by images of him lying next to her with those sexy boxers and tee-shirt off, images of her hands scrabbling over his chest, her body hot and willing, opening up to him like a flower slowly unfurling. 'Of course I don't! You've been the perfect gentleman.'

Because you don't find me attractive...

Why, oh why, had she embarked on this excruciatingly awkward conversation?

'Good. Because you might be a very desirable woman but, as you've correctly pointed out, I'm the perfect gentleman.'

'Desirable?' Kate squeaked.

'I hope I haven't embarrassed you but honesty, I feel, at all costs.'

'That's…ridiculous.'

'Interesting way to respond to a compliment…'

His voice was a husky murmur, burning through her composure. Dante could feel it. He liked it and he was frustrated with himself for liking it, was keen to get things back on solid ground. He loathed the way this woman made things shift under his feet and he couldn't help thinking that it must be the novelty of her, her freshness, aligned to the peculiar situation they'd found themselves in.

'I would never have guessed at your background.' He moved the conversation along even though he knew that he should be ending it. Ending it would have been easy enough—he would have just had to briskly remind her of the hour, fake a yawn and turn his back to her. 'Must have been difficult, making friends, seeing things through.'

'What do you mean by that?'

'Boyfriends… I got the feeling during the course of the evening that your parents worried that they might have been depriving you of a social life they felt you deserved.'

Kate cringed. He'd been listening intently during dinner, head tilted to one side, charming but not dominating the conversation, allowing her parents to confide all sorts of things, because they had absolutely loved him. If she had hoped that he might not be paying attention, that he might have his thoughts focused elsewhere—rather than on what she imagined must have been a boring litany of childhood highlights from her devoted parents—then it seemed she'd been mistaken.

'It's—it's late,' Kate stammered. 'We should get some sleep. I'm sorry I—'

'But we're up now, and I don't know about you, but I'm wide awake. It's going to be a little awkward if we both now lie here in silence pretending to be asleep, don't you think? Besides, where's the harm in a little conversation? All those questions I should have thought to ask?'

Kate's head was spinning from his accidental compliment. *Desirable?* No one had ever called her that before—ever. She contemplated the awkwardness of them both lying next to one another feigning sleep, both knowing the other was wide awake. Had there been any need to point that out? Now it was all she could think about.

'I suppose now that we're up…'

'My point exactly. Of course, if you'd rather we get dressed and sit on the sofa to chat…'

'No. I'm perfectly…comfortable right here.'

'Sure? Earlier, you seemed to…'

'I may have overreacted.'

'So tell me about your parents. I'm getting the impression you thought this meeting might have been slightly different.'

Kate gave in. The more skittish she was, the more ridiculous she felt. The harder she tried and failed to keep her cool, the more she realised how essential it was to do so. 'Okay. I guess I never thought that they would… I'm not sure how to put this, Dante, without sounding rude…'

'Hesitant about speaking your mind? Once upon a time I thought that might have been the person you were. I was wrong. Shall I pre-empt you? You didn't think that your parents would approve of me. Maybe you thought they'd be polite and then wait for the right moment to ask you what the hell was going on? You didn't expect the photo albums and the scrapbooks. Also, maybe you thought that I might disapprove of *them*.'

So he was on a bed with her—big deal.

And what if he said that he thought she was desirable?

That little throwaway remark, so softly murmured, was the spanner in the works. But there was no need for him to know how she felt about him, was there? That would be to open a Pandora's box filled with all sorts of danger.

Her heart sped up at the thought of it. She wondered what that sort of *danger* might feel like. What it might taste like. She'd spent so many years knowing that security was the thing she wanted most. Why did the notion of playing with fire now feather through her, stirring excitement?

'Well?' Dante prompted and she blinked, surfaced and groped her way back to reality.

'I thought they'd have trouble accepting you,' she confessed, voice hitching as she shifted her gaze to stare beyond him to the shadows and angles of the space they were sharing. 'They've been hippies all their lives. They've never placed any importance on material stuff. You're the complete opposite of them and it never occurred to me that—'

'That they might actually find me likeable?'

'I warned you I might sound rude,' Kate said uncomfortably. 'And, yes, if you must know,' she added a little defensively, 'I was also afraid that *you* wouldn't get along with them.'

'Because...?'

'Because, when two worlds collide, it can sometimes be difficult.'

'You might say that about us,' Dante murmured. 'Although *collision* seems a dramatic interpretation. We're in this but you still can't get past finding difficulties everywhere. Relax.'

'I couldn't be more relaxed!' Kate protested tensely.

'Liar.' His voice was soft and amused.

His dark, velvety, accented voice made her shiver.

'You don't understand.' Kate detected an edge of desperation in her voice and cleared her throat, badly wanting to leap out of the bed, but well aware that to do so would bring up more tricky questions and rouse more curiosity than she could deal with.

'Understand this—instead of focusing on all the differences between us....and, yes, there are differences...try focusing on the positives.'

Dante shot her a brooding look from under his lashes. He had said all the right things but the feel of her on the bed next to him...not relaxing. Not at all. He'd never been ruled by his body and cold logic told him that he wasn't going to allow that to happen now. One of them had to take charge, had to be cool and composed, and it fell to him to be that person. The fewer complications that were introduced into this arrangement, the better, and any sort of sexual undercurrent was a complication.

But never had Dante wanted complications more than he did right now. Never had he just wanted to give in to the demands of his body—to go with the flow. Should he have told her that he found her desirable? Too late to retract that statement.

'I guess…'

'We get along,' he expanded huskily. 'We'll learn how to circle one another and deal with situations like this, which are trivial.'

'Trivial…'

'And when it comes to the fact that we're from different backgrounds? Just remember that that doesn't mean that I'm cut off from the reality of what other lives might look like. Like I've explained to you, my life hasn't exactly been a bed of roses. We both bring different things to the table, but none of that affects the practicalities of this deal. It works on a lot of levels and let's put that at the forefront instead of undermining it with potential pitfalls. Make sense?'

'Perfect sense.'

Well, that told her.

How many times did one person need to have cold water thrown over their head before they got the message?

And Dante's message was loud and clear. Bypass the occasional flattering observation, and any casual shows of intimacy purely driven by a need to keep up appearances, and what she was left with was a guy reminding her that this was a business proposition. So why the constant analysing, the *ifs, buts* and *whys*? In the big scheme of things, as he'd said, this was trivial.

She'd edged away from him, and of course he had immediately done the same, but the bed was small. She could breathe him in. Her eyelids fluttered, her nostrils flared and her eyes locked with his.

And still…she wanted to return to what he had said, when he'd let slip that he found her desirable. Why? Was it a case of flattery going to her head? She was so inexperienced. Was that it—that she just didn't know how to deal with this particular unknown? A sexy guy found her attractive and she just couldn't let it go, but wanted to worry away at it as though it were a shaky tooth?

The silence settled between them and Dante fidgeted. He was picking something up and, while he didn't quite know what exactly that *something* was, he was damned sure he didn't want to deal with it. Did he? No! He had shut the door on having to deal with emotions in any woman after his marriage. He had become adept at steering liaisons in just the direction he wanted, out of harm's way. He didn't need complications!

'What you said earlier...' Kate breathed.

Dante caught on fast to where she was going with this and killed it dead before it could develop roots and start growing. 'No need to tread over old ground. I was being honest with you for a reason.'

'I know,' she said on a deep breath and in pursuit of an honest clearing of the air between them. 'You must think that I'm very disingenuous but—'

'There's honestly no need for us to go down this particular road.'

'But there is. I think so. We can skirt round stuff but—'

'I didn't see the point in pretending that I was immune to your appeal,' Dante told her bluntly. 'You're an attractive woman. You just have to look in the mirror to see that.'

'You've never said anything like that before.'

'I have strict codes of behaviour when it comes to people who work for me,' Dante said shakily. He cleared his throat. 'I don't see an attractive woman and find myself compelled to pursue.'

'Well, I actually *do* still work for you in a manner of speaking...'

'Slightly different job title. Look, maybe I'm noticing things about you now because—'

'Because?'

Dante was fast realising that her directness wasn't confined to asking him questions about himself that he signalled he'd rather not answer. She dug in her heels and, it would seem, was happy to brave his displeasure over any and every matter she wanted to clarify.

'Novelty? Who knows, Kate?'

'Novelty…'

She had no idea what sort of women he really found desirable but she imagined that they wouldn't be slight and unremarkable with barely-there breasts and no hips or curves to speak of. So, yes, she got the novelty value aspect, but it hurt.

'And, if there's any kind of reciprocal situation with you…'

'Reciprocal situation?'

'You get where I'm going with this.'

'Ah. Yes, I do. I may be a little uncomfortable around you, Dante, but I think that's understandable. I don't have your level of experience. For a start, I'm a lot younger and I haven't been married. It would be unnatural if it was all water off a duck's back, wouldn't you agree? So, if I seem a little gauche, then that's why—and not because I'm suddenly finding you attractive because of the novelty of it all. That's not the person I am.'

'No?'

'Not at all,' she said stoutly. 'Anyway, I'm fully awake now.' She slipped off the bed. It was cold with the heaters off and the lack of body warmth hit her. 'I'll go read for a while, and in a bit I'll go to the house—let them know that you won't be here for long…'

Over the next day and a half, Kate realised that she knew less about her parents than she'd thought.

How could she ever have thought that they would disapprove of Dante? Because he was mega-rich, mega-powerful, uber-traditional and they were completely the opposite?

Had they actually been waiting for a suitable guy to appear in her life, a man with whom her father could bond? Because that was how it felt to Kate.

Her dad ignored all her dismayed protests that Dante really probably didn't have time to have lessons on self-sufficiency, to be shown every square inch of the land her parents were cultivating or to be treated to an hour's worth of prime viewing of the innumerable photos of the beloved motorbike that was no more.

He was a busy guy and had to leave to return to Milan, she had said more than once the evening before, but Dante had just turned to her with a smile and said that he could spare the time. Angelina was having a fantastic time with his uncle and a couple more days there wouldn't hurt her. He was chatting to them both every day, doing video calls. Angelina was unspeakably excited and preparing some kind of surprise for them when they returned—what it was, he knew not what, but hints were that it was of a culinary nature.

'It's important to get to know the parents of my future wife,' he had said sanctimoniously—which Kate had felt made her sound mealy-mouthed and petty, wanting him to leave when he was happy to stay on for a short while longer, especially given the weather.

Her nomadic, unconventional parents were far more conventional than she had ever given them credit for, Kate realised.

Her mother excitedly pulled her to one side so that they could discuss wedding dresses.

'We always wished we'd done it properly,' she confided, which was news to Kate. 'But we were young, and in a hurry, and both sets of parents were making noises about going to university and getting jobs like everyone else, and we just wanted to escape and have fun and see the world.'

Dante was oblivious to her concerns. He was the perfect fiancé and loving the role. If he was bored by her father's reminiscing, and by all the detailed plans afoot for growing what was at the moment just a cottage industry, then he gave no indication of it.

Not only that, but in the quiet of their quarters he was also the perfect gentleman. He'd taken the sofa, even though she'd assured him that there was no need. It had become quite clear that her novelty value on the desirability front had run its course and that what was being established now was a pattern of friendship that she knew she should welcome.

But, in some strange way, she felt as though she'd been outmanoeuvred and she hunkered down under the duvet, fulminating, while he quietly caught up on work in the tiny living area. The snow had gone from blizzard to a steady, thin fall and she could hear a stiff wind outside blowing it against the windows.

'Why are you sulking?'

Wrapped up in her thoughts, Kate started at the sound of Dante's voice, because she hadn't heard him pad across the floor to the bed.

She flipped onto her side and then wriggled up as he sat on the bed with her.

His gentle voice said he was about to dispense some friendly, anodyne words of wisdom and she didn't want any of it. She was fed up with the Mr Nice Guy image.

'You've taken over,' she said bluntly.

'What are you talking about?'

'This isn't how it was supposed to go.'

'What did you have in mind?'

'It doesn't matter. I don't want to talk about it.'

'I want you to.'

'Why?'

'Because I don't like the thought of you being unhappy. If you have a problem, then spit it out. I can't stand feminine wiles.'

'I'm not unhappy, Dante, and I'm not the sort of person who has feminine wiles! Which is very sexist, as it happens.'

'You're disappointed that your parents like me?'

'I'm disappointed that they've obviously been desperate to see me married off. I always thought they'd want me to be as free-spirited as they'd been.'

'They said so?'

'Not in so many words.'

'You're not your parents, Kate. Their dream was to see the world. Was that your dream?'

'No.' She sighed with frustration, half-resenting his kind voice, which was getting on her nerves the more she heard it. 'It was never my dream. Why are you being so nice to be, Dante?'

'I like you. I like your parents.' He shrugged. 'Is there a problem with that?'

'No problem.'

'Talk to me.'

'Isn't that what I'm doing?'

'I'm not your type,' Dante heard himself say in a roughened undertone. 'And what's the big deal if I'm being nice? Since when was being nice a crime?'

He raked his fingers through his hair and felt the silence pulse between them like a heartbeat. It was cold inside, even though the portable oil heaters were still doing their duty. This was the most basic place he had ever stayed in in his life, and yet the love that had obviously gone into preparing it for them had managed to turn it into one of the best.

He had anticipated a day or two of making a polite effort to advance the fiction of their love story but he hadn't anticipated the feeling of utter relaxation that had overwhelmed him in this small, back-of-beyond place where the bad weather never seemed to end.

This was the feeling he'd used to get as a kid when Antonio had breezed in from one of his adventures—a feeling of playing truant from the daily grind of doing his duty.

'Well?' he challenged. 'If you don't like me being nice, then what would you rather?'

'Nothing.'

'Would you like me to fit into the category you feel safest with—maybe be cold and remote, robot-like? Isn't that a description you once used?'

'Dante…'

'If I stop being *nice*,' he ground out in a driven undertone, 'Then you might not like the person you end up having to deal with.'

'What person is that?'

'A man who can't get you out of his head. A man who still finds you incredibly attractive and is finding it harder and harder not to touch you.'

'You—you don't mean that,' Kate stammered. She rested her hand flat on his chest. He was still wearing his jumper and jeans, and she was fully clothed in her thick pyjamas, but she could still feel the hot burn of his skin against her hand. He covered her hand with his. Somehow he was lying next to her and they were facing one another. She wasn't too sure how they had reached that position, but it felt natural, a feeling of calm after turbulence.

'Trust me. I never say anything I don't mean.'

'But you're not my type.' Kate clung desperately to a familiar mantra. 'And I'm just a novelty to you. You said that! This is just something that suits us both.'

'You're right on all those counts.'

Kate caught her breath in sharp, gut-wrenching disappointment.

'But…?' She found that she was hoping for a *but*.

'What would you like me to say? And you still haven't answered my question. If you don't want *nice,* then what would you rather?'

'But being attracted to one another…that's not what this is about.'

'If I touch you, would you still say the same thing?'

Kate's eyelids fluttered. She thought she heard herself whimper, because his words were so provocative and filled her with such crazy yearning that her whole body seemed to go up in flames.

She felt she should stand firm, but instead she

clung to him, fingers curling into his jumper, a hand seeking the hardness pressing against her. With no experience at all, her body just seemed to know how to behave and what to do, propelled by a craving she had never had before, had never suspected existed.

'I don't know what I'd say! It's not a good idea... None of this is a good idea...'

'You're the one who started this conversation, so why isn't it a good idea?' He talked as his hands began a slow exploration of her, taking his time to feel the outline of her slight body under the heavy-duty pyjamas. He drew in a sharp breath as he slipped one hand under the top and felt the silky smoothness of bare skin.

'I can't think when you're doing that.'

'That's good.' He buried his face into her fragrant hair and got high on the scent of her, then nuzzled her ear lobe before trailing kisses along the side of her cheek and covering her mouth with his. 'I want you so badly right now, I feel as though I'm going to explode, and if that's what novelty does to both of us, then what's wrong with trying it out for size? Sometimes doing something that doesn't make sense can feel very, very good...can turn out to make the most sense in the world...' He pulled back.

'Convince me,' Kate breathed, eyes dark with desire as she pushed her hands under his jumper.

'We both know the score. I'm not cut out for the emotional business of loving anyone. I don't have it in me, and maybe I never did, but you're the opposite. You want the real deal. But in-between both those opposing poles, my darling, is a world of enjoyment to be had because there will be no strings attached.'

'No strings attached...' Kate liked the sound of that and he was right. She wanted love, kids and a 'for ever' commitment, but why not enjoy this blip on the horizon? What would be the point in being a martyr? Wouldn't it be all the more dangerous to deny this crazy attraction? Wouldn't that just feed it?

She was a novelty to him, but wasn't he exactly the same for her? He certainly didn't fit the image she had for any guy she would ever spend her life with. In her mind, her 'for ever' partner would be calm and steady as a rock; a nice, reliable guy who'd make her feel comfortable; a guy who wouldn't send her nervous system into freefall every time he looked her way. Why shouldn't she enjoy the thing that was not destined to last?

'Fun,' Dante murmured, his voice oozing honeyed temptation. 'We could have fun. Nothing lasts, and the great thing is that neither of us has a problem with that.'

Nothing lasts...

For them both, no, not this. This wouldn't last. That was all part of the deal.

'I want fun,' she said simply.

She lay back and breathed in deeply, her body an open invitation, and Dante was overwhelmed by a swoop of pure passion that made him tremble.

Nothing had ever felt better. He touched her gently under the top, then slowly unbuttoned it, then reared up to gaze down at her. Her small, exquisite breasts were tipped with nipples that were perfect tan discs. The thin light filtering through from the living room cast shadows over her and he felt he'd never seen anything so perfect before.

He braced himself on one arm to unzip his trousers but everything was moving too slowly. Shorn of his usual grace, Dante vaulted upright and realised that he was so excited that he could barely get off his clothes. He stripped jerkily, tossing them on the ground, and feeling the pinch of cold in the air. His brain was telling him to slow down but his body was accelerating at a pace he couldn't control.

He clenched his jaw hard and reminded himself that he was a guy with years of self-control bred into him. But when he subsided onto the mattress, and when his eyes caught the hot, drowsy gaze of hers, those years of self-control were washed away and he fumbled to undress her like a horny teenager, stumbling in his efforts and stopping to touch.

He couldn't get enough. He tugged down the pyjama bottoms and she wriggled in a frantic effort to free herself, as hungry for him as he was for her.

'I want to go slow,' Dante muttered shakily, half to himself. He breathed in deeply and touched her gently. He circled her nipple with the tip of his finger, round and round, until the stiffened bud throbbed against his fingertip. He kissed her—not hungrily, even though he wanted to, but gently and tenderly, taking his time and trying hard to ignore the demanding pulse of his erection.

Every touch was a thrill that was wondrous to Kate. Her body was alive for the first time in her life, opening up for this man, leaving her no time to think about anything but the pleasure of sensation.

He stroked the length of her body and she shuddered and clung to him, her nails digging into his shoulders and her legs splaying apart. Between her thighs was a dampness that made her restless and impatient for him to take her...to fill her.

How would that feel? Would it hurt? In the dim recesses of her mind, she knew that her virginity might be a stumbling block, but there was no way she was going to start a conversation about it, not when she was on fire and desperate for him.

Why would he find out anyway?

He covered her nipple with his mouth and suckled on it, drawing it in and firing her up even more as he licked it with his tongue until she was breathing fast and moaning, soft little moans she barely recognised.

Touching her, Dante felt attuned to her every move and every small whimper. Her body was slight, responsive and as delicate as a gazelle's; her thighs opening for him were slender and silky and, when he cupped her mound with his hand, he felt the wetness of her arousal.

'I can't believe how turned on I am right now.' He groaned, blindly reaching for his wallet, feeling for protection without moving away from her heated body.

'Me too,' Kate admitted. 'I just want you to keep touching me. I… Is this okay for you? I mean… I don't have a lot of…'

'Shh… Perfect. Couldn't be more so.'

He set himself the pleasurable task of exploring every inch of her body with his hands, fingers and mouth.

On an unbelievable high, Dante delayed what his body longed to do. He parted her slick opening and dipped his tongue to swirl it around the sensitive bud of her clitoris, and she squirmed against him, angling her body to take full advantage of what he was doing.

When he finally tore open the little packet and sheathed himself with a shaky hand, he was no longer a man in control of his body. He entered her with one long, hard and supremely satisfying thrust. Through a haze of soaring sensation, and even as her own body took flight with his, he was aware of her brief flinch and the sharp little exclamation that accompanied it. But all that was lost in a tide of utter satisfaction and he came with a long shudder, rearing up and swearing with pleasure under his breath, feeling her own body arching up to match his.

Dante fell back, spent. He couldn't remember a more satisfying experience but, then again, it *had* been a while. He'd never been a guy who lived at the behest of his libido. The last time he had slept with a woman had been over three months ago.

'What was that all about?' He flipped onto his side to look at her and manoeuvred her so that she was facing him. He brushed back her hair, enjoying the silky length sifting through his fingers, and patiently waited for her to answer. 'And don't try and pretend that you don't know what I'm talking about.'

'I told you I wasn't experienced,' Kate mumbled as colour climbed into her cheeks.

'That's a little different from being a virgin, wouldn't you agree?' Dante questioned gently. 'Why didn't you warn me?'

'Because I didn't want you to get cold feet,'

Kate blurted out. 'You…you're so experienced, Dante. I knew that if I said anything you'd be turned off.'

'Are you mad, woman?'

'I don't expect you fancy yourself a teacher when it comes to sex.' Kate was lost in defence of her decision, unaware of the soft stroking of her arm or the sudden stirring of his arousal against her belly. 'I expect your days of that are long gone and I was just so… I…'

'You were so hot for me that the thought of me retreating before I could satisfy you was too much to bear?'

'Something like that. Maybe. Yes. I guess…'

'I've never slept with a virgin before. Kate, in all your years travelling with your parents, growing up in a liberal environment, how is it that you never became involved with a guy?'

'Mum and Dad might have led an unconventional life,' she returned honestly, 'But it was never a case of "anything goes". I guess it's a bit like Antonio. He might have travelled around and chosen adventure over duty but look at where we are now… In his soul, he's as conventional as my parents. He was happy enough to let you get on with things but, the minute he thought he was facing his own mortality, all those traditional traits in him came out and he couldn't face the thought of you not settling down.'

'*Touché,*' Dante acknowledged thoughtfully.

'But, aside from that, it was difficult. Difficult hanging onto friends and difficult experimenting with boys.' She smiled and grimaced at the same time.

'And here we are,' Dante murmured with a lusty, satisfied smile. 'And believe me when I tell you, you being a virgin? Not a problem.'

Why did that feel so good? he asked himself. *So oddly good but also....so oddly dangerous.*

Because she was soft and romantic, with no hard edges to protect her from people like him— tough guys with no illusions, cynical on the subject of love.

Drifting this way and that, replete and foolishly contented, Dante pulled himself up short and reminded himself that fun often came at a price. The last thing he needed was for her to find out down the line that the price was too steep to pay. Her reasons for doing this were hard-headed, but that wasn't *her*.

No illusions—that had been the deal. Was there any need to remind her? How often did she have to have it confirmed that love was not in his repertoire?

Why over-egg the pudding? Too much thinking about precautionary measures would be self-defeating.

'In fact,' he ground out, 'It's so much not a

problem that I'm already getting hard for you in record-breaking time.'

'Me too.' Kate sighed and curled into him, nudging her thigh between his legs, already heady for an encore, but he smiled, kissed the tip of her nose and edged back.

'Not yet.' He cupped the nape of her neck. 'Too soon to have me in you again...but, if you like, I can think of many ways to pleasure you without penetration. Would you care to sample what's on offer?' He swept his hand over her breast and oh, so gently, stroked her nipple. She moved closer, her heat melding and matching his.

'Yes, Dante. I rather think I would.'

CHAPTER NINE

DANTE LOOKED AT his wife-to-be with brooding intensity. This was a sight he never failed to enjoy and, ever since they had made love, he had been enjoying it solidly for three weeks.

She was getting dressed. The way she moved, with such grace, never failed to arouse him and that was something he had only just about got used to. He was a man who was easily bored, and that was something he no longer bothered to question, but he wasn't bored now, not nearly.

'You should come back to bed,' he drawled, propping himself on one elbow and looking at her with intense interest. He patted the mattress and watched as she ignored him, searching for clothes which had been scattered in haste on the ground.

She was grinning. He could make that out in the shadowy darkness of the bedroom. It was a little after eight, and the shutters and heavy voile panels only allowed slivers of light through, even though outside the day had already begun.

He couldn't believe that he was here, in a luxury

riad in Morocco for three nights. Since when had Morocco ever been on his list of desired holiday destinations? Actually, when had he ever had a list of desired holiday destinations anyway?

But Kate had laughingly mentioned Morocco, had mentioned that it had always sounded so glamorous when she had been travelling around with her parents, absorbing information like a sponge and dreaming of seeing places without the headache of living in and out of boxes.

And, without bothering to think, he had got his PA to book the most luxurious place in the foothills of the Atlas Mountains, nestled in Berber territory. Every stick of furniture and every artefact in the spacious suite had been hand-sourced from Indonesia, India and North Africa. They had had a veritable sermon on the subject the evening before, when they had been shown to their over-the-top luxurious quarters. There was an infinity pool and they had their own magnificent plunge-pool.

Dante had been tempted to tell the enthusiastic lad that the marvels of the décor and the hand-picked furnishings were irrelevant, when his eyes were only programmed to linger on the woman standing next to him, quivering with excitement.

'Do you ever think about anything but sex, Dante?' she said lightly, slinging a tee-shirt over her head and slipping into some discarded knickers.

'It's very hard when I'm around you.'

'There's a ton of things we can do.'

'I'll bet you can't interest me in any of them. Or maybe just one...'

'We can go hiking. It's stunning here—breathtaking. The mountains...the greenery... Do you know there are even peacocks in the grounds? It's amazing.'

'How do you know all that?'

'I read the blurb in the information pack in one of the drawers. There's the hiking, there are day excursions to explore the area, there are cooking courses...'

'You can forget that particular one,' Dante said drily, reluctantly abandoning the bed but not bothering to get dressed. 'I'm not interested in doing something other people are so much better at doing for me.'

'Lazy.' But her eyes darkened and she stood still, appreciating the raw, masculine appeal of the guy strolling towards her, totally uninhibited and at ease with his nakedness.

He smiled slowly and she blushed and tried to unscramble her whirring mind. 'You are *not* going to distract me,' she said in a muffled voice, but the closer he came the faster her body revved into fifth gear and, when he stopped in front of her, breathing had become a challenge.

'Sure about that?' He eased her towards him, their bodies pressed close, and guided her hand to his erection.

He pushed off the clothes, just. The tee shirt was half-on, half-off, one shoulder exposed, pulling against the soft smallness of her breast. As she caressed him, he played with her nipple, teasing it until she was moaning, head thrown back, eyelids fluttering.

She was definitely distracted.

'Wait…' he murmured. 'I think you're distracting me more than I promised to distract you. That wasn't part of the deal…'

He lowered himself and knelt at her feet, easing down the underwear, which she stepped out of and then gently parted her legs and surrendered on a sigh of utter bliss as he dipped his tongue…

Her whole body quivered under the devastating impact of that hot caress. Her fingers curled into his dark hair and her mind went blank. Each flick of his tongue carried her higher and higher until she was tipping over the edge, flooded with pleasure and ecstasy, and then slowly coming down from that high to a glorious feeling of contentment.

When she opened her eyes and looked down at him, gazing at his dark head, never had she felt so at peace in her life before.

A wave of confusion rolled over her.

She knew excitement when she was around him, a feeling of living life on the edge and trying out stuff for the first time. Being *alive* for the first time as a woman.

But this peace? Her heart was thumping as she drew back with a wobbly smile.

'That was very bad of you,' she teased shakily. She cleared the fog in her head and things settled back into place.

'In which case,' Dante murmured silkily into her ear, 'Maybe you'd like to punish me later...?'

He heard the ping of his phone with another work message and ignored it.

He was getting good at doing that. He had another couple of days here, and so what if he took some time out and temporarily put work on hold?

'So we've agreed to scrap the boring cookery class,' he drawled. 'I'm amenable to an excursion but only if it's followed by a dip in our plunge pool, dinner served in our rooms and all sorts of fun afterwards. Deal?'

Kate burst out laughing. 'Deal.'

'Have you missed Angelina? Milan?' Kate sneaked a teasing sideways glance at him as they were settled into their first-class seats, ready to leave paradise behind and return to pick up where they had left off. 'Your work?'

He was staring at his laptop and she wondered whether she was already losing him as he returned to his punishing schedule. She didn't want that.

He glanced at her, shut the laptop and looked at her for a few silent seconds.

'Of course.' He paused. 'There's only so much time a person can take off work before the backlog piles up.'

'Don't you have people you can delegate things to?'

'In times of emergency, I have things that can be put in place.'

Those times of emergency had yet to materialise. He'd always been the guy in charge, first of his own affairs, and now the affairs of the family empire. He only casually supervised it, leaving the nitty-gritty to his uncle and the comprehensive bank of CEOs who worked alongside him. They were paid enough, after all—too much to be relieved of the majority of their duties because he was a workaholic who hated to delegate.

He had spent so much of his life harnessed to doing what had to be done. Was that freedom? In the process, he had drifted away from his daughter, always too busy to be emotionally and physically available.

He had this window to set things straight on that front, and why shouldn't he take it? The window wasn't going to remain open for ever. There was a limited offer on this particular deal.

Dante didn't believe in any sort of long-term relationship. He had once hoped for something that would at least offer functionality and a certain amount of predictable calm, but he had been wrong on all counts with Luciana.

He wasn't cut out for the hype and he liked the woman sitting next to him. He liked her, respected her and fancied her. She deserved a lot more than a guy who could never give her the life she dreamt of. But he could give her huge sums of money with which to help her parents, and he could give her hot sex until the time came when that side of things fizzled out.

As it would. When he couldn't emotionally attach, there would be nothing to replace the first flare of heat. It wouldn't turn into anything deeper. It would just disappear. He was sure that, when that happened, they would be on the same page.

By then he would have lost this peculiar craving.

'That said…' he murmured, his voice inviting her to lean into him, which she did.

'That said…?'

'I'll be perfectly honest with you, Kate. I feel closer to Angelina than I ever have and I see a chance for me to spend more time with her.' He sighed. 'You've somehow managed to broker a valuable meeting ground between us and I don't want to lose that.' He shrugged. 'I suppose I've been victim to the cliché that it's way too easy to get involved in work to the exclusion of everything else.'

'That would be really great, Dante.'

'So, when it comes to my lifestyle of working all hours and snatching a bit of leisure time whenever and wherever I can? That, at least for the while, will be a thing of the past.'

'Angelina will really love that.'

'Of course, nothing is set in stone. There will be times when I have no choice but to go abroad, to work into the early hours…'

'Of course.' The loose, carefree feeling of drifting on a cloud was beginning to seep away. This sounded like the sort of formal speech a boss might give his secretary at her annual appraisal. She'd feasted her eyes on him in shorts, tee-shirts and loafers on their glorious escape to Morocco. Now, although he wasn't in a suit, he was in dark trousers and dark jumper and he already looked every inch the aristocrat he was.

She didn't know what she'd been expecting and was disappointed that she was disappointed.

'And then there's us,' he murmured in a lazy drawl, his dark eyes roving over her in a lingering inspection.

On cue, her eyes got slumberous with heat and her thoughts turned to the sinfully erotic. Despite the busyness of boarding going on around them, she still had to fight the urge to touch him. It was as though her newly awakened body knew no limits, was greedy for more, like a beggar at a banquet.

She also knew that he could see exactly what sort of effect he had on her, and yet she was helpless to prevent her body from responding.

He shifted so that their heads were together in intimate dialogue. 'When you look at me like that, I feel like getting off this plane right now and heading for the nearest hotel, motel or frankly anywhere where there's a bed and a door I can lock...'

He drew his finger over her parted mouth and looked at her with amusement. 'You have such a transparent face,' he said with a slow smile.

'I'm not sure that's a good thing,' Kate returned with heartfelt honesty. In fact, she was uneasily aware that it very much was *not* a good thing. '"*And then there's us*". What did you mean by that?'

Dante drew back but his eyes were still pinned to her face. He patted her leg and said crisply, 'I hadn't planned on this situation happening but, now that it has, I don't see any reason why we can't carry on having fun until—we're no longer having fun. At least, until we're no longer having fun between the sheets. We're both adults, we've discovered that we want one another...*a lot*...and we're going to be husband and wife.'

'Or we could just put the whole thing behind us as a...blip.'

'A blip?'

'Something that shouldn't have happened.

Something that should be nipped in the bud because of complications that could arise.'

'What sort of complications?'

'Things have a way of turning messy,' Kate said vaguely. 'Don't they?'

'They won't turn messy. We both know the lay of the land.'

Dante marvelled at the rapid turnaround from when he had first laid down the rules of engagement. Then, the thought of sleeping with this woman had not featured on his horizon. Even when he had curiously begun to toy with the notion that she was a heck of a lot more attractive than he'd originally thought—when his thoughts had gone from '*no way*' to '*what if*?'—he had *still* been resolute in his stance. No sex and no muddying of the water.

Now? A three-hundred-and-sixty-degree turn.

'Besides…' He picked up his argument because he was intent on persuading her out of whatever doubts she seemed to have. 'Do you honestly believe that it'll be easy for us to lock the doors between us and pretend that nothing happened? Don't you think that there might be just the tiniest amount of awkwardness? Worse, has it crossed your mind that, the harder we try to fight this, the more it'll grow until it becomes an obsession?'

'I never knew you were so dramatic, Dante.' But she was frowning and what he said took root and mushroomed into various scenarios, all of which had poor outcomes.

Guiltily, she knew that she was also tempted to listen and agree because she wanted him so badly.

'You do that to me,' he said huskily and she sighed and lay back, eyes fluttering shut. She didn't pull away when he raised her hand to tenderly kiss the sensitive underside of her wrist and, when she slid her eyes to meet his, they both knew that she would be his.

With plans swiftly moving forward for a wedding that was getting increasingly close, Kate should have been in a place of relative calm.

They were getting along. They were finding that they had a lot in common, despite their very different backgrounds. The once remote, cold and forbidding man was now a guy who was witty, thoughtful and way too clever for his own good. He liked the way she argued with him and she enjoyed the way he listened and then pulled so many facts and figures out of the bag that she usually ended up scrambling to even up the debate.

And, of course, the sex—it was red-hot.

So why was she uneasy as the date for the nuptials was set and preparations put into motion?

Everything was straightforward. Wasn't it?

Standing in front of a floor mirror she was putting the finishing touches to her hair. When she looked over her shoulder, she caught Dante's gaze and smiled.

'Where's Angelina?'

'Flower arranging,' he returned wryly. 'She went out in the garden with Lorenzo and persuaded him to cut a dozen flowers for her to present to the invalid, although, from the sounds of it, the invalid is in remarkably good form.'

'He still hasn't said what's going on with his tests.' She looked at Dante. They were in his suite and she could see his reflection in the bank of mirrors to one side as he did up the buttons of his shirt. 'Why on earth is he being so secretive? Do you think he's concealing something from us?'

'He would never be as jolly as he's been for the past couple of weeks if there were clouds on the horizon,' Dante mused, reaching for a black cashmere V-neck jumper and slinging it over the white shirt.

He was idly appreciating the curve of her slender body as she angled her head to put on some earrings, tear-shaped diamonds he had given her a handful of days ago, personally chosen.

'Let me help,' he murmured.

He felt the silken softness of her skin against his knuckle as he fiddled with the earring, and he felt something else—the steady drumbeat of the unfamiliar. Was this what domesticity felt like? Was this what hope felt like? The familiarity between them was so easy that words were almost superfluous. Was this what *normality* felt like?

His mouth tightened. Once, briefly, he'd hoped for normality. Marriage to Luciana might have been arranged, and he might have approached it with acceptance of the inevitable, but underneath the cynicism hadn't there been *hope*? Hope that he might find something beyond what his parents had had? She had been a beautiful woman and, at least in the initial stages, vibrant and fun.

It had been an illusion and the hope he'd briefly nurtured had withered and died fast enough. Whatever small shred of optimism he'd ever had, about having a wife who might be more than a woman with the right pedigree, programmed to fulfil the duties into which she had been born like his own mother, had disappeared. That was not for him, and it was better that way, because there was nothing more painful than the loss of hope.

He didn't like the taste in his mouth now and, thinking about it, neither did he like the urgency of his body whenever he was near this woman.

Did she make him weak? Maybe not, but it felt like it, and he loathed that and rejected it out of hand because he knew what it could spell—a loss of control, a dismantling of barriers.

'The dress suits you.' He spun round on his heels and sauntered over for his wallet and the keys to his car, which he had intended to drive himself rather than use a car with a driver. Now, though, the romantic, exhilarating trip felt over the top and unnecessary. He needed to recover his perspective and romantic, exhilarating car trips, even with a mini chaperone in the back seat, weren't exactly a great starting point.

He needed a breather, by which time everything would have fallen right back into place and this moment would be lost to reality.

'I think I'll get Paolo.'

'Your driver? But I thought you wanted to take your car out for a spin?' Kate smiled. 'Weren't you the guy who made a big deal about never having enough opportunity to drive the cars you own?'

She had turned to look at him and he returned her laughing, open gaze with a shuttered expression.

'I've suddenly remembered I've got work to do,' he said abruptly. He scrolled down his phone without looking at her, but *feeling her*, and hating the thought that he might be hurting her with his sudden change of attitude. However, more pressing was his urgency to get back onto solid ground.

When he finally did raise his eyes, something inside him clenched because there was confusion in her gaze, although she was still smiling, her fingers fiddling with the diamond necklace round her neck.

'Okay.'

'I've taken a hell of a lot of time off.'

'I know.'

'Companies don't run themselves.'

'You don't have to justify working in the car, Dante,' Kate said gently. 'I don't expect you to give up the day job because playing truant suddenly looks more appealing. I *know* you have work to do. Besides, when Angelina gets tired—and I'm sure she will on the trip there—she gets fractious and enjoys playing games and being entertained, so I expect I'll be busy doing that.'

'Good.' He wasn't sure how much better he felt but so be it. He waited politely by the door, still scrolling through his phone while she hurried to get all her various bits together, and when he did finally rest his dark gaze on her he swiftly stifled the rush of adrenaline at the sight.

She was as dainty as a fairy and as graceful as a ballerina. Expensive clothes suited her, made her look even more feminine and ethereal than she already was. He felt the sluggish heat in his veins and the stirring of a libido he found so hard to keep in check when he was near her.

'We should get going.' He turned, opened the bedroom door and stood aside for her to waft past him, brushing against him in a way that was unconsciously provocative.

Then he put distance between them, which was easy, because when they got outside Angelina was skipping and waiting, half-hidden behind a massive bouquet of flowers, while behind her Dante's head gardener smiled and lifted his shoulders in a resigned, indulgent gesture.

And in the car he sat in the front seat, opened his laptop, closed the partition between front and back and waited for feelings he couldn't fathom—but needed to banish—to subside.

CHAPTER TEN

WHAT WAS GOING ON?

Kate wasn't sure. Dante worked for the duration of the long car trip to Antonio's palace while she half-focused on an exuberant Angelina, who had an exhaustive supply of car games she wanted to play.

Had she said something? Done something?

Or was it just her imagination playing tricks on her? The truth was that the past few weeks had been utter bliss. She had never thought that they could blend so seamlessly, that their personalities could be so complementary. How could she ever have put him down as someone as chilling as winter sun?

She desperately wanted to find out but it was only after they'd finally arrived, after coats had been removed and discreetly taken away, and Angelina disappeared with Antonio and the flowers, which she insisted required immediate attention, that Kate was able to tug Dante to one side.

'What's wrong?'

'Wrong?'

'Have I said something?'

Their eyes met, hers anxious, his cool and un-readable.

'Not that I can think of,' Dante told her, moving out of the hall and heading for the sitting room, where pre-dinner drinks were being served.

Kate hesitated and tugged him to a stop, and felt the way he stiffened with a sinking heart.

Panic clawed inside her.

And hot on the heels of panic came the appalling realisation that she was hurt. She felt the gentle shove of being pushed aside and that *hurt*.

No, more than *hurt*. It sent her into a dizzying, frightening tailspin because somewhere and somehow she had been stripped of her defences.

Being in control—an adult having fun with no strings attached and no expectations—had been washed away under an onslaught of emotions, desires and wants that she had never predicted.

She had done well to recognise her own limitations, to acknowledge her lack of experience, so why on earth hadn't she made the logical leap to realise that those very limitations would leave her horrendously exposed when it came to dealing with a guy like Dante—would leave her *heart* horrendously exposed?

They had slept together, and she had been foolishly infected by his assurances that it was all some fun which would run its course, leaving no one hurt.

So what happened now?

She fixed a smile on her face while her thoughts continued pelting along on the runaway train.

'Good. And did you get much work done?'

'Enough.'

'Enough for what?'

Dante met that soft, sexy, questioning gaze and resolve slammed into place—no misunderstandings, no blurred lines. They'd slept together and he wanted to carry on sleeping with her. It was unthinkable that they wouldn't, because they enjoyed one another way too much to walk away from the physical side of the arrangement.

Unforeseen, but now impossible to ignore.

That said, ground had to be recovered. He'd wavered, found himself over-thinking the whole situation, and now was the perfect moment to gather himself and get the splayed deck of cards back in a stack, ready to be shuffled and dealt, but this time with him firmly in control.

He growled, stepping towards her, invading her space and breathing her in, her scent the headiest of aphrodisiacs. 'Enough for me to spend some undiluted time in bed with you later. No distractions. Just me and you, and me doing all sorts of sexy things to you.'

'Dante…'

'Shh…' He traced her lower lip with his finger. 'Let's not get wrapped up thinking too hard about this.'

'What do you mean?' Kate whispered.

'I mean, you were upset because I had to work in the car.' He pulled back and watched her with steady, cool eyes.

'I wasn't upset.'

'I'm not in the business of putting work to one side to cater for any kind of relationship.'

'We talked about this! I know that.'

'Do you?'

'Of course I do.' She drew in a deep, shaky breath. 'I know the limits of this situation.'

'That's good.'

'You've repeated the rules and regulations often enough to make sure I don't forget.' Her voice was terse, her body rigid with tension.

'Yet sometimes amnesia can kick in when the rules get a little tweaked, and us sleeping together comes under that category, wouldn't you agree?

Kate lowered her eyes. Her heart was beating wildly inside her as the cold ramifications of her misjudgement coalesced.

She fallen in love with a guy who was only capable of lust. She'd given herself to him hook, line and sinker and now she felt sick at the prospect of the future yawning ahead of her. She saw a slow-motion scenario of Dante losing interest: turning his back on her because she'd outlived her novelty value; having discreet liaisons, which was what she had foolishly agreed to when everything had seemed clear cut.

'I suppose so,' she said faintly.

'But now we've cleared the air.' Dante pulled back. 'We'd better see what's happening with my daughter and my uncle and the flowers.'

'Which looked a little tired after the car journey here,' Kate chipped in, because a chirpy remark seemed to be expected of her. Sure enough, Dante nodded with an approving smile and turned, and she edged a little away but kept pace as they headed to the sitting room.

They could hear voices before they entered— Antonio and Angelina. She would have to keep up the front. Could she? She smiled all the way through a long early evening and then, when Angelina was in bed, through an even longer dinner. It was just the three of them, with a menu that never seemed to stop, and every delicious course tasting like cardboard.

Thank the lord, Dante knew how to hold court. If she hadn't been so tense, she would have been amused at the way Antonio bristled at every question to do with his health, which he'd repeatedly done ever since they'd returned to Italy, until Dante was forced into retreat. She would have been amused at the way this big, powerful, aggressively dominant male could be manoeuvred into a position he obviously didn't much like.

She would have stared in rapt fascination at the guy she had fallen in love with, would have hung onto every word and would have been utterly involved in every aspect of the conversation, because that was just what happened when you loved someone.

And, most of all, her head would have been filled with thoughts of what was going to happen when they headed upstairs, when the clothes came off and desire took over.

'Are you feeling all right, my dear?'

Kate blinked. Somehow the drinks had disappeared. Where? Had she actually drunk the glass of dessert wine that had been pressed on her? She hated dessert wine. And where was Dante?

'Sorry?'

'You're a million miles away. Have been all evening.'

'Where's Dante?' Kate blinked, owl-like. Antonio's eyes were narrowed, watching her shrewdly.

'Sent him off.'

'Sorry?' Conscious that she was repeating herself, Kate tried to get a grip. How on earth could she have been thinking of Dante and the sudden mess she was in all evening and yet literally not even have noticed when he left the room? 'Where?'

'Work.' Antonio shrugged. 'Told him I had unearthed some problems in the shipping sector of the company. Looked thorny. Urgently needed him to cast an eye. He seemed pleased enough to take the bait.'

'Bait?' Kate frowned, but she found it impossible to join the dots in the conversation because her brain felt foggy.

'You do not look like a radiant bride-to-be, my dear. Ever since you returned from seeing your parents, you'd been bursting with happiness. But now…?'

'No, no. Not me,' Kate said with dismay. 'I've been my usual self.'

'So what is going on here?' Antonio waved aside her feeble response. 'Have you and my nephew had an argument? To be expected. These things happen. Pre-wedding nerves, I believe it is called, although, having never been in that place myself, I can only speculate.'

'Antonio…'

Yes, she'd been brimming over with happiness, she thought miserably. She'd been floating on cloud nine but now she had crashed back down to earth and without any safety gear to cushion the fall. Every part of her was hurting and underneath the hurt was the dreadful fear for what the future might hold.

It would be fine because it would have to be. Her eyes started to well up and she looked away, but she didn't trust herself to speak, and into the telling silence Antonio prodded gently, moving to sit closer to her and covering her hand with his.

'I have seen it all,' he murmured in a voice that could have melted ice. 'You can tell me anything. Are you pregnant? Is that it?'

'No!' That managed to bring a smile to her lips. 'Now that *really* would be a disaster,' she murmured to herself. The smile didn't last. It faded when she thought of how Dante would greet an accident like that—with horror. His worst nightmare.

'Ah.'

Antonio rose unsteadily to his feet to move to the door, brushing away her helping hand, but then turned back round and reached for his phone.

'I see how the land lies, my dear,' he said sadly.

'I don't think you do, Antonio.'

'As I said, nothing comes as a surprise to me any longer, but perhaps there are things left to surprise *you*. You and my nephew. Who will be here in a minute—I have texted him. Told him I need to see him urgently.'

'Why?'

Antonio shrugged. 'Perhaps it is time for an old man to stop causing mischief…'

He sat them down.

Out of the corner of her eye, Kate noted Dante's wary expression. She wanted to reach out and squeeze his hand, share amusement at his uncle's dramatic antics, but everything had changed and that sort of spontaneous gesture no longer seemed carefree and innocent.

'I am afraid I have been guilty,' he said heavily, 'Of a small amount of well-intentioned deceit.'

'Meaning?' This from Dante, sitting next to her on the sofa and maintaining just enough distance to remind her that they were not the loved-up couple she had ended up deluding herself into believing they were, but two people who had simply enjoyed having sex within a relationship in which they'd both given themselves permission to do so without over-analysing.

'I *did* have a genuine scare.' Antonio huffed defensively.

'Meaning?' Dante repeated, voice considerably cooler, while Kate blinked and did her best to follow the trajectory of what Antonio was saying.

'I *thought* I was at death's door— that was perfectly understandable, and I will not have anyone say otherwise!'

Dante got there before her and flung himself back with a groan that was somewhere between frustration and despair.

It took Kate a little bit longer. She had to hear a bit more of the explanation before she got the gist of what Antonio was actually saying and then, just in case either of them had missed the glaringly obvious, he stated in defiant summary, 'Can anyone blame an old man for wanting to leave his house in order before he meets the Grim Reaper? Can anyone blame me for trying to steer my beloved Dante into a relationship that would benefit both him and Angelina—incidentally, the apple of this old man's eye? If it happened that I exaggerated the health crisis facing me, then could anyone blame me?'

He made a show of mopping his brow. 'I suppose, if we are all going to have a Spanish Inquisition about the whole thing, I would admit that I could have said sooner that my cancer scare turned out to be an infection, happily taken care of with the right medication.'

He flapped his hand dismissively while Kate digested this startling announcement. 'That's good,' she ventured faintly into the ever-increasing silence.

'But,' Antonio continued as implacably as a steamroller now that he had embarked on his comprehensive confession, 'I felt in my gut that you two...would work.'

He gestured with Italian eloquence but his eyes were sad. 'I admit that I knew it was a contrived relationship to keep an old man happy. I do not know, and nor do I wish to know, what sort of agreement you reached, but I was very happy to encourage you both. I was so certain, you see, that love would follow in the footsteps of convenience.'

He shot Kate a sidelong, knowing look.

'Things have not, however, lived up to expectation.' Another elaborate shrug as he rose to his feet. 'To conclude, there is no need for you to continue this pretence. I am fine, and it would be better to break it off before time and fate decide to cause even more mischief than I have.'

Kate was hardly aware of him shuffling out of the sitting room. The revelation had struck her like a blast of freezing air and had given her a choice in what happened next.

She was free to walk away without a guilty conscience and, more to the point, so was Dante.

She half-turned to look at him and met dark, inscrutable eyes before he vaulted upright to pour himself a whisky from the bottle that was sitting on a silver tray on one of the coffee tables.

'So,' he drawled. 'An evening to remember.'

He remained where he was, standing, sipping the whisky and looking at her over the rim of his glass. 'But it's a good thing that he isn't as seriously ill as we thought…'

Her head was swirling. She couldn't meet the brooding intensity of his gaze but things were getting clearer in her mind. Antonio had said what he had said for a reason. He had seen right through her to the love that had grown out of nothing, thriving on promises of happiness that had never been made.

She was at a crossroads now.

Give it all up—the money and the hopes for her

family, because there was no way she would accept a hand-out for duties unfulfilled—and know that at least she would be walking away from slow, painful heartbreak before she served out her two-year contract.

Or breathe in deeply, keep her fingers crossed that she could maintain a front and look at the bigger picture, which was the very thing that had inspired her in the first place.

Or another option…

'Agreed.' She cleared her throat. 'Dante…'

'I'm not entirely sure what my uncle was hoping to achieve with his extraordinary confession, aside from the very important purpose of putting our minds to rest on the health front. Certainly, from my point of view, it's business as usual.' He shot her a devastating, wolfish smile that made her blood grow hot.

'Perhaps for you,' Kate said quietly. 'But not for me.'

'What are you talking about?'

'This isn't going to work. I should be able to get back to where we started, get back to where *I* started, but I can't.'

'Let's not over-think this,' Dante said roughly, strolling towards her and swamping her with his proximity as he sat next to her and reached to lace his fingers through hers. 'My uncle may have dropped a bombshell, but nothing has to change, and this situation still makes good sense.

The traditional members of my family are appeased and, far more importantly, my daughter has a guiding hand for the next two crucial years of her life before she moves on to boarding school.'

'I'm in love with you.'

The silence that met this bald statement was deafening. His face had become a closed book and he moved his hand and sat back in stunned silence, giving her ample time to feel queasy.

'If I could be on the sex-with-no-strings-attached page, if I could think about what we have ending and turning into something else until the expiry date comes up, then I *could* carry on. Because I do need and want the money and will never accept any of it if we part company...'

'If...'

Going for broke, Kate breathed in deeply and said huskily in a rush, 'We get along so well, and I don't just mean in bed. As two people, we laugh and chat, and sometimes it feels as though we're *one*. Do you feel any of that? Do you feel that we might make a go of this?'

'What are you talking about?'

'We could...really see what happens, Dante. I know you've been burnt in the past and I... I've never thought that you were the kind of guy I could ever go for, but we could both be brave... see where this takes us for real.'

She saw his answer in the way he sprang to his

feet and the speed with which he put distance between them until he was staring at her, narrow-eyed, from across the width of the room.

'That is not an option,' he said with unyielding ferocity. 'It never was and it never will be. You knew the rules of this…arrangement.'

'So I did,' Kate said sadly, rising to her feet, thankfully more steadily than she'd feared.

And also…relieved.

'Of course, I won't take anything that came with this deal,' she said, tilting her chin. When he brusquely told her not to be ridiculous, and to expect him to pay her exactly what he'd promised whether or not the contract had been fulfilled, she replied as hard as glass, 'I won't be accepting a penny from you. If you make the mistake of sending money to me, expect it to be returned to you immediately.'

She walked towards the door and paused, then she glanced over her shoulder at the drop-dead gorgeous guy who hadn't budged from where he had fled on the opposite side of the sitting room. 'It's been fun. I'll pack as soon as I head up, and perhaps you could get your driver to return me to Milan. I'll be gone by the time you get there. And say goodbye to Angelina. She's very precious and, just for the record, you'd be a complete idiot to ever think about sending her to boarding school.'

Final piece said, she let herself out, and within

forty-five minutes she was on her way to pick up the pieces of a life she'd spent the past two years building.

She left a pool of cold behind her.

Dante hadn't budged as she'd shut the door behind her. He'd remained as still as a marble statue, his body wired and rigid, knowing that she was upstairs getting ready to go.

And of course there was no option! On cue, he had called his driver and ensured that his car would be ready and waiting to return her to Milan.

She was right—she would be gone by the time he got back there. Indeed, he knew that he could stay on for longer in Venice with his uncle, giving her ample time to clear off before he returned.

Love? No. Hadn't he made it perfectly clear that that wasn't on his agenda? Hadn't he told her more than once that theirs was a working relationship and nothing more, even if sex had been introduced into the equation, an addition that neither could have foreseen when their plans had been made?

He wanted his life run on clear-cut lines. His marriage had been a failure and had shown him the nature of his limitations which, deep down, he had already known. Emotions and the messiness that accompanied them were not for him.

Hadn't he told her that, more than once?

If she had chosen not to listen, then so be it,

but now that the pact between them had been broken, and an impossible gauntlet thrown down, he had no choice but to let her go. Disentangling the whole business would be annoying and inconvenient but not beyond the wit of man.

Angelina would be bitterly disappointed, but she would recover, because children did that—they recovered.

All those thoughts raced through Dante's head as he eventually got moving and sat on one of the chairs, nursing a glass of whisky and scowling at a turn of events he hadn't anticipated.

Was this his fault? Had he led her on? Taken his eye off the ball and given her hope for something more where there was none?

He'd said all the right things…

But had he *done* all the right things?

He stared down into the amber liquid, swirling it in his glass, trying to think, but it was suddenly like wading through treacle.

His thoughts wanted to go somewhere but he could no longer direct them, and they drifted in his head, disconnected and just out of reach of interpretation.

Time would sort this edginess out, he decided. And he would send the money to her. What she chose to do with it would be up to her but, having met her parents and bonded with them, it was the very least he could do.

It was several hours later before he fell asleep, half a bottle of whisky to the good.

Kate knew that she was dithering. She'd been so tired after that drive back to Milan. Dante's driver had been waiting for her, not that she'd needed reminding of how keen Dante was to see the back of her now that she'd become too hot to handle with her declaration of love.

She should have slept in the back of the car but her head had been buzzing. One minute, she'd been as high as a kite and elated that she had been brave enough to tell him how she felt, and them immediately after plunged into the cold depths of misery as a future without him had loomed ahead of her in all its cold reality.

Which meant that she'd been exhausted by the time she made it back to his villa in Milan. Exhausted enough to have fallen asleep, fully clothed, on her bed.

Not *his* bed, which she had shared for so many glorious nights, but hers, the bed she should have stuck to before adventure had beckoned and she had thrown caution to the winds.

She woke with a fuzzy head, disoriented, and for a few seconds wondered where the heck she was and what was going on. Weak sunlight was streaming through the windows because she hadn't bothered to draw the curtains.

Realisation of what had happened hit home with

the force of a sledgehammer, galvanising her into action.

What an unholy mess. That was all she could think as she flung things into the suitcases she had brought with her from England.

She didn't want to think about Dante. She didn't want to think about anything. She couldn't begin to contemplate the nightmare she had left him to deal with when it came to retracting the engagement they had only just announced.

She had to sift through the finery to pull out all her old stuff, depressingly shabby and cheap in comparison, with her head all over the place. It was only when she had dragged her cases down and was about to head to the kitchen to grab some coffee that she heard the thunderous sound of a helicopter.

Dante's helicopter.

She recognised it from those rare occasions he had landed on the specially designed bit of land at the back of the villa. Like many uber-wealthy Italian aristocrats, he had helicopters at his disposal, although he seldom used them because of environmental reasons.

What the heck was he doing back here?

She needed time to run away!

But, if she couldn't have that, then she needed time to gather her forces. He would have been called back on urgent business and with any luck she could avoid him altogether. She couldn't imagine he wanted to say anything to her or even see her.

But as she lay low in the kitchen, aware that he would spot her bags by the front door when he entered, she was braced for a confrontation as she heard the sound of his footsteps on the marble floor.

And then there he was.

So tall, so impossibly handsome. She struggled to breathe and had to make her way to one of the leather chairs by the table and sink into it whilst dragging her eyes away and focusing on her coffee.

He looked terrible. Good. Maybe he'd at least reflected on the road ahead that would involve him wriggling like a worm on a hook when he was forced to explain away the vanished engagement.

She couldn't imagine him wriggling like a worm on a hook.

'I'm sorry.' She broke the silence to look at him as he remained standing in the doorway. 'I didn't expect you to return so quickly or else I would have left earlier. I've already packed, as you've probably seen. My suitcases are by the front door. I'll finish my coffee and be on my way.'

'Kate…'

'No!'

'No what?'

His voice was haggard. 'Have you been drinking?'

'Maybe a little.'

'And you *flew* the helicopter?'

'Would that worry you?'

Sudden rage consumed her. How could he just show up here and have this devastating effect on her? Yes, she knew, of course she did, but she still resented the love that made her vulnerable.

'It would worry me if anyone was stupid enough to do anything that could endanger their life and other people's lives while under the influence of drink.' Her voice was cool.

'My pilot got me here.'

'I'm going to go now.' She pulled her phone out to call the cab company she always used, and when she next glanced up it was to find that he had covered the distance between them and was standing in front of her, his hands resting on the back of the chair which he had pulled out. 'I don't want you here,' she whispered shakily.

'I know you don't but... What you said...'

'No! I refuse to discuss that. I said what I said and I'm not going to go over it. Why would I? You've made yourself abundantly clear on the subject of not wanting me in your life.'

'Can I sit down?'

'It's your house.' But as she began to stand, a response to him sitting down, she froze because he reached out to circle her wrist and memories of his touch flooded through her with blistering force.

'You told me you love me,' he rasped. 'I was a fool to push you away.'

Kate glanced at him, torn between dragging her hand away and listening, and then hating herself for being tempted to listen.

'I'm not listening.'

'Please.'

She hesitated. He was the last man on the planet to beg for anything but there was a plea in his dark eyes that cut through all her defences.

'You have five minutes.' She shrugged off his hand, folded her arms and stared at him in unwelcoming silence.

'That'll do.' He raked his fingers through his hair. 'You know so much about me. More than anyone ever has. I never realised how much I'd told you over time about myself or how comfortable I'd become in your presence until—until suddenly our familiarity with one another hit me, winded me, scared me.'

He sighed. 'I'd never had that before. Even with my parents there was a formality that we never managed to breach. I think somewhere, somehow, I'd hoped that I might find *normality* with Luciana, find that elusive thing that seemed to make marriages tick...' He smiled sadly. 'And, when my marriage ended in disaster, I shut the door on those hopes for ever.'

'Yes,' Kate acknowledged with painful honesty.

'I concluded that I wasn't capable of love, and more importantly would never again delude myself into believing that it might exist for me, for someone like me.'

He gazed at her with such tenderness that she was disoriented. Even in the depths of their passion, when real life had disappeared under an onslaught of wild craving, she had never seen what she saw now.

She wanted to talk. She remained silent.

'I never knew that it would sneak up on me like a thief in the night, steal all my ramparts and leave me exposed. Kate, my darling, when you told me how you felt, I obeyed the instincts that had been driving me for most of my life. I pushed you away. And then I drank too much whisky for my own good and pretended that, when it had done its work, I'd open my eyes and find that nothing in my life had changed. Find that you were gone, but I'd be on track, because no one had ever thrown me off-course before.'

'And?'

'I thought of you coming back here...packing your things just like you've done...and the thought was so unbearable, I couldn't sit still. I couldn't breathe. I felt like I was suffocating under the weight of thinking that I might have lost you for ever.'

He paused and shot her a crooked smile that was filled with so much emotion, her heart felt fit to burst. 'So here I am. Begging your forgiveness and telling you that the thing I want most in life is to be with you, to share my dreams with you and…most importantly…to not feel scared of a future of giving my heart to the woman I love. So…will you marry me, my darling? For real?'

Moments like this, Kate thought in a daze, were made to be bottled.

'There's nothing in the world I would like more, my love…'

* * * * *

Were you captivated by
Unveiled as the Italian's Bride*?*
Then make sure to check these other
Cathy Williams stories!

Hired by the Forbidden Italian
Bound by a Nine-Month Confession
A Week with the Forbidden Greek
The Housekeeper's Invitation to Italy
The Italian's Innocent Cinderella

Available now!